ORACLES OF THE MOTHERLAND

WOLE DARAMOLA
&
TOLU ODUNLAMI

authorHOUSE

AuthorHouse™
1663 Liberty Drive
Bloomington, IN 47403
www.authorhouse.com
Phone: 833-262-8899

This is a work of fiction. All of the characters, names, incidents, organizations, and dialogue
in this novel are either the products of the author's imagination or are used fictitiously.

Published by AuthorHouse 12/01/2022

ISBN: 978-1-6655-7482-2 (sc)
ISBN: 978-1-6655-7480-8 (hc)
ISBN: 978-1-6655-7481-5 (e)

Library of Congress Control Number: 2022920469

Print information available on the last page.

This book is printed on acid-free paper.

Because of the dynamic nature of the Internet, any web addresses or links contained in
this book may have changed since publication and may no longer be valid. The views
expressed in this work are solely those of the author and do not necessarily reflect the
views of the publisher, and the publisher hereby disclaims any responsibility for them.

ACKNOWLEDGEMENT

First and foremost, I am most grateful to God for giving me the vision; and the opportunity, strength and guidance to achieving this goal of mine.

My deepest appreciation to my lovely wife, Eniola, who has been supportive throughout the entire process of making this book a reality; and to my two delightful children, Analise and Jeremiah, thank you for being my source of motivation to accomplish this book. I hope I have made you proud.

To my mother, thank you for creating the road-map that led me where I am.

To my siblings, thank you for your unwavering supports through my entire journey.

To my parents-in-law, thank you for your love and support.

To my co-author, Tolu, thank you for your brilliant and creative ideas on this book.

Wole Daramola

I'd like to thank God for the ability and foresight to write this book, and as someone with several near-death experiences, including during the development of the book, He alone takes all the glory.

I'd also like to thank my wife, Kim, who has been with me in the toughest of times, an ever present and reliable pillar on my journey through life.

Lastly, I'd like to thank friends and family who provided encouragement and served as sound boards, and Wole my co-author who broached the idea of writing a book.

Tolu Odunlami

DEDICATION

I dedicate this book to my father, late John Afolabi Daramola, who supported and encouraged my love for art and storytelling since I was a little lad.

Wole Daramola

I dedicate this book to my mum, who was my first English teacher (she actually was an English teacher), she provided the foundation of reading and writing which carries me to this day.

Tolu Odunlami

CONTENTS

CHAPTER 1

Reborn in the Forest

In the days of old, nestled inside the three-quarter circle formed by the Omíshàn Mountains, lay the Odùduwà kingdom, located along the western part of the Guinea Coast. It consisted of villages and towns like Sàbẹ, Ìlóbù, Etí-Òsà, Olókìtì, Lánipèkun, Ìjèbú, and Èjìgbò, and tributary kingdoms such as Dahomey, Hawani, and Ashanti. The mountains reached into the heavens, and clouds danced on their peaks. The rain traced paths down the sides, etching a unique signature on each incline. The winds slapped the outer slopes of the majestic mountains, periodically rushing into the crevices and creating a singsong whistle.

The seven streams that converged at the center of the kingdom rushed out to catch the fishermen on their way out to sea. They could not have cared less about the wind and its playful ways.

In the Odùduwà kingdom, every person was accountable to the next; there was little difference between commoner and nobility. Strangers greeted each other with the familiarity of brotherhood, and sisters took care of one another's kids. It was a beautiful oasis, preserved by a cultural utopia that was little known to the rest of the world. But just like the regal mountains that Odùduwà was built on, the kingdom had a crack; it was almost imperceivable, but nonetheless, it was there.

The time of the yearly cocoa festival had arrived. The young men would go into the outer forest and gather the choicest cocoas to bring back for the women to make *musu*, a sweet chocolate pie that was intoxicating. It was so sweet that many babies would enter this utopia nine months later. The young men bristled with excitement, waiting to commence their annual competition.

The young men would spend a day deep in the forest with the guidance of elders and warriors and seven days camping in the open terrain, learning the rules of manhood and proving themselves worthy to be called one.

The young women giggled as they huddled in groups. They would compete to see who could make the best musu. The better it was, the higher one's chances of getting a husband. It was also shameful for the family of any young woman who made terrible musu; she and her mother would be to blame, and suitors would be wary.

Adélolá, the queen of Odùduwà, hurried into the royal courts, her dress sweeping the floor elegantly. Her beauty and sense of style were a thing of legend. She wore a tasteful yellow, blue, and green *ànkará* dress, with blue beads adorning her neatly braided hair and white beads around her long neck, wrists, and ankles.

Adélolá's maid, Lúlù, was the most sought-after among the maids. Eligible bachelors of the land adored her because of her beauty. She was from the village of Sàbẹ. She walked a step behind the queen, carrying her purse. Lúlù was dressed in an equally elegant *ànkará* dress that was tailored to her curvaceous body and thick backside. She was also adorned from head to toe with white beads that complemented her dark shining skin. They were a sight to see.

Many princes had asked for Adélolá's hand in marriage when she was a princess of the Etí-Òsà ruling house. A few suitors had dueled, and Prince Àjosè, now the king, had been the lucky one. Some said he had been chosen by the gods.

Lúlù kept pace with the queen. Her round, attractive face was covered in painted patterns, and she scowled at anyone who did not immediately acknowledge the queen. She had raw sexuality about her, familiar to women of the outer forest who ate yams and palm oil and drank coconut water.

King Àjosè, dressed in a royal *dàshíkí aso-òfì* and loincloth, stood to greet his queen. "Lolá, my dearest, how are you this fine morning?"

Queen Adélolá sat in her chair and huffed in exasperation. "How am I doing? The drums I requested are nowhere to be found, they have not yet gathered the flowers and palm fronds, the decorations are a mess, and where are my dressmakers? I cannot possibly wear the same clothes as last year!"

"You worry too much, my dear," King Àjosè replied. "I have never seen a cocoa festival turn out badly. Besides, there is enough food and palm wine to satisfy the entire kingdom for days."

"That is easy for you to say," the queen retorted. "Men are so easily satisfied. You are not involved in the planning and—"

The king reached down and kissed Adélolá. He was a strikingly handsome Black man, tall and muscular like a horse, with a beard that had a life of its own.

The queen's anxiety melted away.

Lúlù smiled. That was the end of the conversation.

Kúyè, the chief adviser to the queen, grinned from ear to ear. He was wearing his dàshíkí and *shóóró*. Adélolá's father, the *Ọba* (king) of Etí-Òsà, had assigned Kúyè to her when she married Àjosè. He was the intermediary between Etí-Òsà and Adélolá in her role as the queen of Odùduwà. Kúyè was like an uncle to Queen Adélolá. The queen's behests were paramount to him.

"Àjàmú!" the king bellowed.

Àjàmú was the captain of the king's guard and the general of the Odùduwà warriors. He was advanced in age but was still good-looking, strong, and an experienced warrior. His full beard made him alluring to women, yet he was a man of strict character. He had refused to take another wife after the loss of his wife during childbirth; instead, he had dedicated himself to serving the kingdom. He believed that everything happened for a reason instead of by chance.

Àjàmú was dressed in an open-front, sleeveless, dark brown dàshíkí, exposing his broad shoulders, large chest, and loincloth. Black warrior laces were tied around his biceps, and his cutlass, dagger, and ax were fastened around his waist. He climbed down from his chestnut horse, rushed forward, and bowed before the king. "My king!"

3

"Commence the initiation!" the king instructed.

Dressed in their *dàshíkís* and loincloths—and some in *dàshíkís* and *shóórós*—the elders of Odùduwà prepared for the annual hunt. They gathered the young men and led them to the opening of the forest near the city. Their strides were proud and authoritative.

Most of the young men were dressed like Àjàmú, but the darker shade to Àjàmú's dàshíkí showed his superiority as the general.

The young men were to be taught about manhood, the ways of women, and their responsibilities as men. They would play games, wrestle, practice using weapons, hunt wild animals, and gather cocoas. As tradition demanded, Àjàmú oversaw the expedition.

During the expeditions, Àjàmú always gave a speech that inspired young and old alike. The young men sat in a semicircle with the older men standing behind them, some on their horses. Everyone waited for Àjàmú to speak.

"You are coming of age and must carry the torch that we have carried for all these years. From generation to generation, we have honored our ancestors and preserved the glory of the Odùduwà kingdom. I have fought and bled with my kinsmen beside me, and I have seen the deaths of many warriors. I also pray for the death of a warrior someday." In those days, it was a thing of pride and honor for a warrior to fall in battle.

Àjàní, the son of Àjàmú, dropped his head at the statement. The last thing he wanted was to lose his father. Death had already robbed him of his mother at birth, but he understood the ways of warriors. Dying a warrior's death would make his father a legend.

"Tonight, you shall transition from boys to men. You shall show your skills as fighters and hunters, and you shall bleed with pride. You shall spit in the face of fear, and you shall renew your strength. You are sons of Odùduwà. You shall stand strong and raise your head high in the face of fear. Make us proud!"

"Odùduwà! Odùduwà! Odùduwà!" The chant of the warriors reverberated in the mountains. Fear dissipated as the young men picked up their weapons and charged into the forest in pairs.

Àjàní glanced back at his father before heading into the forest with his partner.

Àjàmú gave a silent nod. In that quick second, volumes transpired between father and son.

Àjàní had his father's approval, and he knew he had better come out as one of the best hunters. Otherwise, he would be a disgrace to his family. With a dagger by his side and a spear in his hand, Àjàní and his best friend, Labí, disappeared into the foliage.

Àjàní and Labí were inseparable. They knew each other well and had their own sign language. It would serve them well in the forest.

At a small pond, Labí signaled for Àjàní to pause. The pair crouched in the bushes with a bow and arrow.

Àjàní whispered, "Let's wait here a while. I am sure animals will stop here for a drink."

Labí nodded in agreement and climbed a tree. "I hope we get something big."

"A big buck would be nice." Àjàní traced a track in the mud with his arrow. "Whatever made this mark would be a good catch."

Hours went by. It was almost time to return.

Labí signaled to Àjàní with a low birdlike whistle. A deer was approaching.

Àjàní stared at the deer across the pond and quietly nocked an arrow. He moved slowly; the deer had keen hearing, and the slightest sound or abrupt movement would alert it to their presence.

It was getting dark. This was their only opportunity to prove their hunting prowess. If they returned empty-handed, they would be disgraced. Àjàní drew on the bow slowly. Labí looked on from the tree, holding his breath. Suddenly, out of the corner of his eye, he saw movement. A leopard was stealthily approaching Àjàní. With all his concentration on the deer, Àjàní didn't notice the leopard. Labí had to make a split-second decision: alert Àjàní and miss the game or wait. Labí kept silent, but he was ready to strike a death blow to Àjàní's predator if it attacked.

Seconds felt like hours as the leopard got closer. Suddenly, the bowstring let out a sharp whistle as the arrow took flight. In that same instant, the leopard leaped in Àjàní's direction. Labí sprang from the tree, clutching the dagger with both hands. The arrow hit the deer as Labí's dagger slammed into the side of the leopard's neck in midair. The leopard let out a sound halfway between a howl and a growl as they both hit the ground.

Labí repeatedly stabbed its neck, shoulder, and side. The seventh stab put it to rest. Labí, breathing heavily and sweating profusely, closed the eyes of the leopard and kissed it on the forehead. The leopard's spirit left its body to reunite with the spirit of the motherland. The first natural law of the Odùduwà culture was to show respect to all things—even the dead.

Àjàní stared at the dead animal in disbelief. "Why didn't you warn me a leopard was about to attack?"

Labí snorted and wiped the dagger on his cloth. "I saved your life."

"Saved my life?" shouted Àjàní.

"If I had told you, we would have lost the deer," Labí stated calmly, still breathing heavily.

"I hope I shot that deer despite all that commotion you caused. You'd better hope it's still there," Àjàní said with a scowl.

"Eh! Look at this ungrateful man! You should be grateful I saved your life—again. I should have let it bite a piece of your backside," Labí replied jokingly.

Àjàní hissed and got up, making his way to the other side of the pond. Theirs was a friendship tried and tested. They were closer than brothers and had a love for each other that many admired. Labí followed closely behind as they came upon the carcass of the impala. They both looked at each other and broke out laughing.

"Àjàníogun, you are a warrior!" Labí said.

"Jagunlabì, you are a hunter!" Àjàní exclaimed.

"You are a true warrior," Labí declared.

"No, *you* are the true warrior," Àjàní affirmed.

They congratulated each other and laughed into the night. Labí picked up the carcass of the deer, blood dripping down his body and loincloth. Àjàní picked up the leopard. They left a trail of blood on the forest floor as they walked toward the camp, laughing and singing. They had entered the forest as mere boys but would emerge as men, the subject of much envy.

The warriors and elders were worried. Àjàmú stood at the edge of the camp with Sóbógun, his second-in-command, staring anxiously into the darkness. Àjàní and Labí arrived at the camp late that night. Upon seeing his son and Labí, he broke out in a smile. They had killed a large deer and one of the strongest animals in the forest. They had the biggest trophies of all the young men. It took everything in him not to run and hug his son.

As they reached the camp, he shouted, "Kneel!"

Their bodies and loincloths were dripping with blood from the dead animals still on their necks. They dropped to their knees.

"Where have you been? What took you so long?" Àjàmú shouted.

Labí glanced at Àjàní. "It would be best if you explain to your father," he whispered to Àjàní, willing him to answer.

"We had to wait several hours, my lord," Àjàní explained. "We did not want to return empty-handed. We were attacked by a leopard but managed to kill the leopard and the deer. We present them both to you, my lord."

They dropped the animals from their necks and looked up cautiously. The general's anger was legendary. He had once slapped Àjàní during a training camp and had disciplined Àjàní's squadron leader for allowing him to get out of line.

Àjàmú surveyed the young warriors in the camp. "This is what we like to see—bravery in the face of danger. True warriors. As I always say, finish whatever mission you are given. Failure is not an option." He returned his gaze to the two young men and nodded proudly. "You have done well. Welcome back to the camp. Rise."

The young warriors roared in excitement.

Àjàní and Labí smiled as they stood up. They had won the competition and the respect of Àjàmú.

The whole village would soon learn of their exploits. Drumming broke out. Warriors young and old began singing the warrior song: "We are warriors, forward ever, backward never, we are warriors, you can't see me coming, I'm light as a feather."

On the last night in the camp, the boys were circumcised as a final rite of passage into manhood. The hut where the circumcisions took place had a smoke duct where smoke signals were sent out every time a circumcision was performed. It was normally preceded by screams and then silence. If you were close enough, you might hear whimpering.

7

The òǵǵǵró, an alcoholic brew that helped to reduce the pain, caused hallucinations. The feeling of being intoxicated and in pain at the same time was indescribable. Four men would hold the young men's limb as the operation was carried out. The young men would start to hallucinate as the òǵǵǵró took effect; many saw spirits of dead relatives and the appearance of various gods. As the hallucinations progressed, they normally got lost in the fear and shock of the visions and forgot why they were lying on the hard bamboo bed with four grim warriors holding them down.

Every young man nursed his fears in a different way. Some closed their eyes and sat under trees, and others huddled in small groups and whispered. Suddenly, a prolonged scream erupted from the hut, and the men saw smoke rings wafting from the duct. They never got used to the screams. Everyone wondered who would be next.

The native doctor shouted from the doorway, "Proceed!"

The young men went cold.

Àjàní looked at his best friend. "Strong, brother, strong."

Labí proceeded to the hut quietly. Àjàní listened intently. A few minutes later, he heard the screams of his comrade. He cringed when he saw the smoke signals. He could almost feel the pain. It would be his turn soon.

CHAPTER 2

Festival

The young men carried their bags of cocoa and danced into Odùduwà in order to prove their manhood.

The women dressed in different designs and styles of aso-òfì and ànkará wrappers, with beads on their hair, necks, waists, wrists, and ankles. They sang and cheered them on.

Showing pain was a sign of weakness and made a man lose his appeal in the eyes of the females. Àjàmú led the procession with the officers and guides following suit. The young men took up the rear, carrying the bags of cocoa.

They proceeded in two files, partially hunkered down in a pose that looked like they were about to attack. They shifted from side to side in sync with the rhythm of the music. Drummers pounded out beats ferociously, young women clapped and stamped their feet, older women let out nasal, tongue-flapping shrieks, and the men chanted, "Jagun Jaagun, hay! Jagun Jaagun, hay!"

The king was waiting to receive them in the palace.

The crowd was whipped into a frenzy as the men proceeded to the village square and then to the palace to meet the king.

In the presence of King Àjosè, the men knelt while the crowd gathered behind them. Àjosè rose and said, "Welcome, Àjàmú!"

"Your Highness," he replied.

"Odùduwà has been waiting for you to return with our sons. Have you made men of them?" the king asked.

Àjàmú replied, "They have lived up to expectations, my king. I present your warriors!"

The young men rushed in front of the king and formed a straight line, setting down the bags of cocoa and the game from their hunt.

The king stood at one end of the line. It was the moment everyone was waiting for. Àjàní looked at Labí; Àjàmú looked at King Àjosè. The entire kingdom gawked from behind.

"Disrobe!" Àjàmú shouted.

Without betraying any emotion, the young men opened their loincloths and let them drop to the floor. In the crowd, murmurs, giggles, and chuckles abounded. The older men looked on as it brought back memories of their own experiences. The young women strained to see what they could, but they dared not cross the line to inspect the men from the front.

Hands behind his back, Àjosè walked slowly in front of the men and inspected them.

Each man emptied his sack of cocoa as the king passed him.

Àjosè did not say a word. After the inspection, he asked who had won the competition.

Àjàní and Labí stepped forward.

"You shall thrill me with your exploits tonight. Tonight, you shall drink with me at my table." He turned to the rest of the young men. "You left as boys, and you returned as men. We shall celebrate your manhood tonight."

The young men felt a mix of emotions. They felt a sense of pride and excitement to transition from boyhood to manhood, but they also felt uncomfortable showing their loins in public.

The king gestured to the young men to pull up their robes. With that, the king repeated the warrior chant. He joined the crowd and started dancing. The drumming and singing resumed, and the crowd cheered exuberantly as they watched their king dancing among them. It was a memorable sight. King Àjosè was loved by his people.

Queen Adélolá shook her head and smiled; he was still as wild and energetic as the first time they met. The young men slipped away, and the older women carted away the cocoa and game.

Dancing and celebration continued late into the night. Àjàní and Labí joined the king and recounted their events in the forest. Àjosè laughed out loud with his people. Àjàmú and Sóbógun sat at the high table with the king, Àjàní, and Labí. The chiefs and the elders were seated at tables around the room as they wined and dined.

Dépò, a strong and respected young warrior with a competitive nature, sat with the other warriors. He wished he was sitting at the high table with the king. He was always in competition with Àjàní and Labí. Even though he had not killed a leopard, he and his fellow warrior had stuck to their plan and came back to camp on time with their own kill. He felt like he had done as well as Àjàní and Labí. He whispered his disdain to a fellow warrior, but he dared not voice his opinions publicly. There was zero tolerance for dissent in the military, and he knew it. Besides, they were all on the same team, and this was one of the few times they would be singularly recognized. The celebration continued until the cocks crowed in the distance.

Morning arrived quietly. The courts were still. One would not have thought there had been a celebration a few hours earlier. The eighth month was a festive month in Odùduwà, and the courts were always busy.

Lúlù rose early as usual. Her place was beside the queen, and she rarely engaged in celebration, especially if the queen was not directly involved.

Queen Adélolá was a graceful and self-respecting woman. She would not put herself in a situation that compromised her dignity. Lúlù respected the queen, and Adélolá loved Lúlù. She was a confidante and a friend to Queen Adélolá. Everyone knew if you wanted an audience with the queen, your best bet was to go through Lúlù. If Lúlù did not approve of you, there was little to no hope you would get access.

Lúlù hurried through the courts and down the royal passage. The Odùduwà palace was massive—one of the largest of its time. It was surrounded with a strong stone wall three feet wide and twenty feet tall. It had solid pillars and imposing gates made out of gold and brass. Massive botanical gardens, natural waterfalls, and a zoo where the animals roamed freely surrounded an immense courtyard. The many rooms of the palace overlooked the striking scenery.

On Lúlù's way to the queen's room, she passed the king's room. The door was ajar, which wasn't normal. She glanced in through the doorway and saw King Àjosè half naked on the bed with his legs hanging on the floor. He'd had too much to drink and had not made it into his bed. She glanced back and forth in the passage. There was no one in sight.

Lúlù entered the room quietly to help the king into bed. The bed was so big that she had to climb halfway in with the king.

A maidservant stepped out of the royal kitchen on her way to the maids' quarters. She noticed the king's door was opened. The maid stepped toward the door to shut it.

"Lolá?" the king said. He was still intoxicated.

"It's Lúlù, my king," Lúlù replied.

"Lolá?" The king held Lúlù's hand tightly.

"It's Lúlù, Your Highness."

He held her hand for a few seconds, and then his arms went limp and fell to his side.

Lúlù stared at the king for a few seconds. Even in his drunken state, he was still such an attractive man.

The maidservant saw all that happened and tiptoed away without closing the door to avoid being seen. She hurried down the passage, shaking her head as she rounded the corner. The maid went to Kúyè, the chief adviser, and told him what she had seen.

"Are you sure of this?" Kúyè asked.

"Yes, my lord. I believe Lúlù is having an affair with His Highness."

"Do not mention this to anyone." Kúyè invited the maid in and shut the door. Kúyè was a middle-aged man who had not taken a wife for himself, but had a weakness for women. He was having affairs with a handful of maids, but all of them were loyal to him.

Lúlù slipped out of the king's room and headed to the queen's room. No one was in the hall.

She knocked on the queen's door. "My queen?"

"Come in," the queen replied. "Come."

Lúlù walked in and sat on the queen's bed.

"Did you see all that happened yesterday?" the queen asked. "This place was a madhouse."

"My queen, you should be used to it by now. This is what happens every year," said Lúlù.

"We didn't have this in my father's kingdom in Etí-Òsà. All these parties. But if the people love it, and this is the tradition, then so be it." The queen suddenly bent over in pain and squeezed Lúlù's hand.

"Is it that time of the month, my queen?" Lúlù asked. She knew the queen had a painful menstrual cycle. It was an open secret that the queen had feminine issues. She had miscarried twice. No one was sure of the cause, but those close to the queen were sensitive to issues involving her reproductive health.

"It is," she muttered. "I hope I won't have to deal with those old superstitious women who suggest all these rituals to reverse this curse on my family and me."

"My queen, maybe it is time you listened to their suggestions," Lúlù replied gently.

"Are you superstitious too, Lúlù? I thought you were cut from a different cloth. I expect ..." Adélolá buckled down again in pain.

"I will call for the physician and priestess, my queen," said Lúlù.

"Get the physicians, but do not bring that old witch near me," Adélolá ordered.

"Yes, my queen." Lúlù hurried off.

The queen spent the rest of the day in bed, and Lúlù coordinated events for the festival.

Deliveries were made from far and wide: food, clothes, décor, and responses to the invitations sent to various kingdoms and dignitaries.

Lúlù came back two days later to check on the queen. She was back to her normal self.

"Things are in place for the festival, my queen," Lúlù reported. "All that is left is your royal touch and blessing."

13

"I am eternally indebted to you Lúlù. You have saved the day once again." The queen smiled and hugged Lúlù.

Lúlù replied, "I owe you many debts, my queen. This is the least I can do."

The queen and her handmaids went to the market to buy items and finalize activities for the annual cocoa festival.

The festival started the night of the full moon in the eighth month. The summer heat lingered into the night, bringing the excitement of nocturnal possibilities. The palace gate opened, and guests filled the court. Acrobats and dancers entertained the guests with prolific performances while they waited for the main event.

Young and old women alike pounded cocoa in mortars, and others stirred musu in large clay pots with large wooden pads. Firewood from the ubiquitous baobab trees crackled under the pots.

One performance stood out. The beat changed and a slow, dark, and rhythmic sound—*putum pa tum tum, putum pa tum tum*—was followed by the shaking of dried beans in a wooden gourd. The background accompaniment sounded like *shikishiki shikishiki*.

A small masquerade dancer rushed into the court, laid a circle with tinder, and set it alight. Larger masqueraders joined the circle and started a slow, animated dance that kept time with the rhythm. They looked menacing, but the show was mesmerizing. The beat picked up, and so did the dancing. The performers let out periodic shouts and growls.

Several of them started hallucinating. They represented the spirits of different deities: Ògún, Sàngó, Òsun, and Obàtálá. The people of Odùduwà worshipped these powerful spirits. Citizens of Odùduwà were highly religious, and there was little separation between the spiritual and the physical. They believed they were a product of spirituality and that the gods had a hand in everything.

Finally, the lead masquerader, possessed by the spirit of Ògún, the god of iron, stood still. He set his eyes on Fádèyí, the traditional head priest to the gods and one of the oracles of Odùduwà. After a few seconds, Fádèyí dropped his stare in acknowledgment of Ògún. The masquerader turned around and slowly looked at the entire court. Each attendee dropped their stare as the masquerader's gaze came upon them. It was said that if anyone other than the high priest looked directly at Ògún, they would drop dead. After making a 360-degree turn, the masquerader collapsed—almost vanishing into the ground.

The other masqueraders collapsed in unison. Honor had been given to the gods.

CHAPTER 3

Successor

Boom! Boom! Boom! The grand cymbals rang out, followed by the bellowing voice of the *alukoro*. The town criers were known for their strong voices and sure-footedness. It was said they could run for half a day without food or water to pass a message to another kingdom.

The royal seal on the alukoro's headgear marked his position and importance. "All stand!"

Activity in the court paused. The announcer's voice brought silence, and everyone stood. "His Royal Highness, King Àjosè, is approaching the throne."

All eyes looked toward the entrance, where the king appeared in full royal regalia. The head of a lion sat on his head, and the skin fell to his neck. Cowrie shells and beads adorned his neck and arms, and a plate adorned with metal and impenetrable leather covered his chest.

The armor, a family heirloom, had been forged by the best ironsmiths from Dahomey. A loincloth and long tassels covered his groin and upper thighs. Intricate leather sandals covered his feet. He was a warrior king, and he came in battle gear to show it. He stood at the foot of the throne and stamped his spear to the ground to signal the beginning of the royal presentation.

The young men who were considered sons of the king filed in and lay prostrate at his feet.

The king stamped his spear on the ground a second time.

"*Káábíèsí o!*" they shouted in unison.

The king held out his arms. Robe bearers removed his battle gear and spear and replaced them with the royal crown and white robe.

"Her Royal Highness, Queen Adélolá!" bellowed the announcer.

The queen walked in, wearing a white wrapper—an elegant wraparound garment—that flowed from the topmost part of her bosom to the floor. Red beads and body paint covered her face, bare shoulders, arms, and feet. She walked into the court to take Àjosè's outstretched hand.

The young ladies rushed into the court behind the young men and knelt on both knees.

Àjosè and Adélolá were loved by their people.

The people bowed their heads in respect. The dignitaries and guests looked on in admiration. Odùduwà was famous for the benevolent relationship between the king and his subjects. Àjosè led Adélolá up the short flight of stairs to the throne.

The people raised their heads and shouted, "Káábíèsí ooo!"

They held the greeting until the king and queen sat down. The guests, who had come from kingdoms far and wide, sat down after the king. Some were benevolent, but others were not so much.

Àjosè's father, Adégòkè, had managed to quell the intertribal wars and competition, and he had brokered a truce among the four kingdoms that surrounded Odùduwà. On his deathbed, King Adégòkè had tasked his son with maintaining the truce among Odùduwà, Dahomey, Ashanti, and Hawani. This had led to the rapid economic and technological advancement of the kingdoms. Attending the cocoa festival signified a continued adherence to the truce.

King Àjosè stood. "Thank you, Your Majesties, distinguished guests, and loyal subjects, for gracing this occasion with your presence. My queen and I thank you, the people of Odùduwà, for making another annual cocoa festival possible. This, like others held in times past, shall mark the beginning of life for many of our young men and women. This time next year, I am sure we shall hear the sound of newborns."

Everyone laughed.

The queen shot a quick glance at Lúlù, and she hurried away from the court. She was going to prepare the queen's chamber for the king. Tonight, Queen Adélolá would make another attempt to conceive.

"We shall soon celebrate the exploits of our young men in the forest, eat the meat they brought, and taste the musu prepared by the young women. I have special gifts for the greatest hunters among the young men—and the ladies who make the best musu. Let the cocoa festival begin!"

A roar went out from the crowd. Music and dancing resumed on the courts. Servers brought an exotic variety of food and drink. There was an unending supply of palm wine. The cocoa festival was in full swing.

The king invited people to speak. He also invited Àjàní and Labí to tell the story of their hunt, after which he presented them with two iron daggers encrusted with the royal coat of arms.

The most significant event of the festival finally arrived. A long table was set in the middle of the court. Seven musu tasters sat down, and seven dishes were placed in front of them. They tasted each dish as the guests watched in anticipation.

The groups that had prepared the musu watched in suspense. Every few minutes, a dish was taken off the table. The group that had prepared the dish was out of the competition; it was not because they did not do a good job, but there could only be one winner.

When the musu dishes were narrowed down to three, they were introduced to the guests. The judges were visibly impaired from the intoxicating musu.

Three royal judges were also introduced. Dishes with the three samples of musu and water were served to the guests.

The royal table was served, and the king coordinated the tasting. "Let us taste the musu from the first group."

Everyone tasted. Guests muttered their approval or disapproval.

"What do you think?"

"Do you like it?"

"This is wonderful."

"Let us try group two," the king said.

Again, there were murmurs.

"Now, finally, group three," said the king.

The people discussed the musu.

"Remember to drink water and taste again if you have not yet made up your mind," the king said. "Now, my distinguished guests and subjects, if you think the first sample is the best, please raise your hands."

One of the king's administrators counted the hands.

"If you think the second sample was best, please raise your hands," the king said. "Now the third."

A quick tally was made, and the result was handed to the king.

"Group two wins!" he exclaimed.

A group of women led by a young maid, Sinmi, came forward.

The queen stood. "These ladies have reminded us about the essence of womanhood and the pivotal position that the women of Odùduwà hold in society. I present to each of you six yards of Egyptian cloth and access to the royal seamstress to sew any garment you desire. I also present you with bronze pots from Egbédá. We are grateful to the king and queen of Egbédá for their friendship and loyalty." She curtsied in the direction of the Egbédá royals.

The women thanked the queen and received the gifts. Egyptian cloth was very expensive, and few people had bronze pots. Clay pots were more common. The women put the pots on their heads and left in single file. It was expected that every woman in Odùduwà know how to balance a pot on their head.

The young men were transfixed by Sinmi and her group. They had fantasies about a future with them.

Dépò and Labí started after the group simultaneously.

Sinmi was from the village of Lánipèkun, north of Odùduwà. She was beautiful, blessed with glowing skin and long hair.

Dépò caught up with Sinmi in a dark corner outside the palace. "My lady!" he shouted.

She stopped. The other ladies laughed and continued on their way.

"I think I need more of your musu," he said, trying to keep a straight face.

Sinmi could tell he was intoxicated.

"There is more in the courts, great warrior," she said sarcastically. She was not interested in Dépò.

"I want the musu from you, my lady." He stepped closer and grabbed her, squeezing her tightly. "I want you to feed it to me. Nothing could be sweeter than eating musu from the hands of a beautiful woman." He started groping her.

"Stop," she said quietly. She did not want to draw attention to herself. "Stop!"

Dépò felt a heavy blow to the back of his head. He released his hold on Sinmi and stumbled, almost blacking out. "What?"

Labí stood over him, glaring. "If you open your mouth, I shall remove your front teeth."

"You take the side of a woman over your fellow warrior?" Dépò asked.

Labí raised his hand to strike Dépò again.

Sinmi reached out and grabbed his hand. "No, please. No need for that. Don't spoil the festivities. This is not the night to fight. Thank you for helping me, my lord."

"Let me walk you home." Labí glanced at Dépò in anger and hissed as they started down the well-beaten forest path. "So, what is your name, my lady?"

"Sinmisólá, my lord, but I go by Sinmi." She smiled.

Labí looked at Sinmi. "My name is Jagunlabí, but you can call me Labí." He placed his hand on his chest and smiled. "Where are you from?" This was his chance to woo the girl he had been interested in since he was a young lad.

"I am from the village of Lánipèkun." Sinmi smiled again.

"Ah, it's close to mine. I am from Olókìtì," responded Labí.

They talked as they walked along.

The festivities continued. Guests and citizens indulged in the musu and palm wine. By now, most guests were feeling the effects of intoxication, and they danced and sang freely. The queen made a point to socialize with all the guests.

The last ceremonial rite of the evening came, and representatives from each of the kingdoms brought a torch forward.

Fazilah, the beautiful princess of Dahomey, came forward and bowed. "Your Highness." She put out the torch, signifying the official departure of the Dahomey kingdom from the festivities. She mounted her horse and rode off with her emissaries.

The prince of Ashanti put out the Ashanti torch. "Your Highness." He bowed to Àjosè, climbed on his horse, and rode off with his envoy.

Princes and princesses who had attended from surrounding kingdoms also came forward, put out their torches, and left with their emissaries and royal family members.

The prince of Hawani came forward, but he was stopped by his father. King Guguwa was a short man with a beard that looked like it had not been shaved in ages. He was dressed in white royal regalia with a white turban and white scarf. He had a short fuse and little tolerance in his dealings. He stood in front of the flame and stamped the floor with his staff.

The court went quiet. Shadows from the flame distorted the king's face; it was a disconcerting image.

"Oh, great King Àjosè, we have gathered tonight as we have done yearly to honor you and your kingdom and keep the accord established by your late father. You have become our de facto leader in this great region, and we honor you as we have honored your father."

Members of the crowd nodded as they whispered among themselves.

"Our princes and princesses, who are our successors, have brought forth our torches and put them out. I ask you now, oh King, where is your successor who will ensure we enjoy continued tranquility in this region?"

"What insolence!" Kúyè exclaimed.

Àjosè gazed at Guguwa and raised his hand, signaling Kúyè to stop.

The crowd went quiet, and all eyes fell on Àjosè.

"These are my successors." He pointed to the young men, women, and warriors of Odùduwà. "In the Odùduwà culture, these are princes and princesses—and the gods shall choose the next king and queen of Odùduwà after my reign."

More murmurs of affirmation came from the crowd.

King Guguwa said, "I ask you again, King Àjosè." He hit the ground with his staff and asked in arrogance, "Where is the child you birthed from your loins to succeed you when you are gone?" He put out the flame, got on his horse, and rode off.

King Guguwa's son and their entourage followed closely behind.

CHAPTER 4

Conspiracy

A few weeks after the festival, Kúyè approached Queen Adélolá in her chamber.

"My queen, a word," Kúyè said.

The queen gestured to her maids to leave the room.

Kúyè stared at the young maids as they walked out of the queen's presence. He was weak when it came to women.

"Please, keep your eyes and hands off my girls," she said lightheartedly.

"Yes, Queen." Kúyè approached the queen. "Your Highness, King Guguwa's encounter with His Highness has been weighing on my mind since the festival."

"Do not mind that ignorant fool," the queen replied.

"I have an idea." Kúyè stroked his jaw.

"I'm all ears, my lord," the queen said.

"My queen, do not be upset with what I am about to suggest," he said.

"Please, tell me." She sought.

"There is a way for His Highness to have an heir," he said.

"How?" she asked.

"I know you are very close to your maid, Lúlù, and I know you trust her," Kúyè said. "If you allow her to get pregnant for His Highness, you can keep her away from the public eye until she gives birth. Then you take the child and raise it as your own."

The queen pondered the idea. "Thank you, my lord. I shall think it over," she said.

Kúyè bowed and left.

Queen Adélolá sat down. She felt overwhelmed with defeat over not being woman enough to give the king an heir. For days, Kúyè's suggestion consumed her thoughts.

A few nights later, King Àjosè could not sleep. He got up from the queen's side while she was asleep and went for a quiet walk around the palace courtyard. He considered the humiliation and the challenge made by the king of Hawani. This year's festival would not be easily forgotten.

The queen awoke to an empty bed in the king's chamber. She looked out on the courtyard.

The king was staring at the moon from the center of the courtyard. *The gods know best,* he thought. *They shall choose the best king for Odùduwà when the time comes. If only I had an heir, it wouldn't be so complicated.*

Queen Adélolá gently touched the king's shoulder and rubbed his back. "And you shall, my king."

The king was startled to hear the queen's voice—and her replying to his thoughts—but he did not mind the back rub. "Adélolá, how did you know I was here?" he asked with a tender, deep voice.

"You're my husband. I'll always know where to find you," Adélolá replied wryly.

"And how did you know what I was thinking?"

"You were talking out loud, my king. Guguwa had no right to disrespect you. I have a request, my king, and I want you to promise you won't turn me down."

He looked at her and smiled. "It is difficult to refuse you anything."

Adélolá cautiously said, "I want us to have an heir through my trusted maid, Lúlù."

"Stop it, Lolá! How could you propose such a thing? I shall not be a part of that!"

"You promised not to turn me down," the queen protested.

"I did not make such a promise, and I do not want to discuss this matter any further!" The king walked back to his chambers.

Queen Adélolá stood alone for a few seconds, lost in her thoughts. Then she walked brusquely into the palace, resolve in her eyes.

Time went by, and a transient calm hung over the Odùduwà kingdom and its surroundings. The new moon had come, and as it was customary, the elders gathered the children around a large bonfire and told stories.

On the last night of the full moon, Queen Adélolá planned a banquet for the king. She sent a message inviting him to join her in the large room normally used for formal occasions.

The king was pleasantly surprised. "Lolá, may I ask what this is all about?"

"My king, you know I like to do something different every year," she said with an inviting smile. She gave Lúlù a nod that only they understood.

Lúlù nodded and stepped out of the room to carry out the queen's plan.

The banquet began with palm wines and traditional dishes from the Odùduwà kingdom, then foreign wines and food from neighboring kingdoms.

Queen Adélolá had spared no expense. She made sure the king's cup was kept full.

The king was pleased. "Lolá, ask me anything you want, and it shall be done without hesitation."

"Lay in my bed tonight, my king." The queen smiled.

The king let out a boisterous laugh. "Is this your request?"

"It is, my king." The queen smiled again.

"I shall roll in your bed for as long as you want!"

The night was far spent, and the king was already drunk. His cup dropped to the floor as he drifted in and out of an intoxicated sleep. At the order of Queen Adélolá, guards carried the king to her chamber.

Lúlù was waiting in the queen's chamber. She wore a revealing gown and the queen's perfume. She entered the queen's bedroom— where the king was already half naked—lifted the veil covering her face, and got in bed with the king.

He barely had his wits about him. His eyes were halfway open as he put his arms around Lúlù. "Lolá, my queen," Àjosè slurred. "You smell nice … as always, now let me … grant … your request." He drunkenly climbed on top of her.

It was a short night. Lúlù got up before the cock crowed at dawn and slipped quietly to her quarters in the palace. The still morning air was laden with secrets whispered through the trees. A few animals had heard the events of the night, but the kingdom was largely oblivious.

The queen was already up, putting on her beads and makeup with the help of her handmaids.

The king walked in with a bright smile on his face. "How is my queen this beautiful morning—and how was your night?"

"I had a wonderful night, my king. I hope you did too," the queen replied evenly.

The king motioned to the queen's maids. "Excuse us for a moment."

"Yes, Your Highness," The handmaids left the room.

"You surprised me last night, my queen. You did things you had never done before—things that reminded me of my days outside the palace. We certainly have to do that again tonight."

"Certainly, my king." The queen forced a faint smile, not sure if she should be glad or upset.

"By the way, where is Lúlù?" asked the king.

"Why do you ask, my king?" asked Queen Adélolá.

"Normally, she would be with you. I did not see her at the banquet last night either."

Queen Adélolá did not make eye contact. "I sent her on an errand; she shall be back soon."

"I have to attend to the elders. They are waiting to see me at the court. I shall see you tonight, yes?" King Àjosè gave the queen a kiss and walked out.

"Very well, my king." Queen Adélolá's head spun, and her mind filled with images. She let out a deep breath.

Later that night, King Àjosè went into Queen Adélolá's room and lay with her. Some nights, when she got him drunk, she would send Lúlù into the room instead. This continued for a few weeks until Lúlù broke the news to Adélolá that she was with child. The queen told her not to tell a soul about this.

Queen Adélolá sent for Kúyè.

"Uncle, Lúlù is with child now," the queen said.

"This is good, my queen," he said. "I shall ensure she does not appear in public from now on."

"Very well," the queen replied.

Kúyè kept an eye on Lúlù and made sure she wanted for nothing. Kúyè became overbearing and started placing restrictions on Lúlù, which made some of the other maids ask questions.

Sometimes, the queen would intentionally walk a few strides behind Lúlù, admiring her newfound glow. She often thought, *Did I make the right decision? Surely the gods have favored me, my husband, and the kingdom. Yes, yes. It is the right decision.* She shrugged off the negative thoughts, but she couldn't flout the sensation of despondency about the inadequacies of her own womanhood.

One evening, Lúlù was stopped in the courtyard by one of the maids. "What did you do to Elder Kúyè?" she asked.

"Why do you ask?" Lúlù asked.

"He is always watching you these days. It's almost as if you offended him," the maid said.

Lúlù did not respond.

"Where did you get all these beads? Look at your clothes—and you smell so good, Lúlù."

"Shut your mouth and mind your business," Lúlù hissed and walked away.

The maid giggled and rolled her eyes.

A few weeks later, the queen felt sick. She decided to take a bath and rest for the morning. As she neared the bathroom, she stopped in the hallway to regain her balance.

"Are you all right, my queen?" asked the maid who escorted her.

Adélolá did not respond. Everything spun around her, and she fainted.

The maid screamed.

Male servants rushed in and carried the queen to her chamber.

The king was informed immediately. He went down to the queen's chamber, accompanied by Kúyè. "Lolá, what happened?"

The queen tried to answer, but she was too weak to speak.

"Your Highness, let us call for the palace's physicians to care for the queen," Kúyè suggested.

The king turned to one of the palace guards. "Call for the physicians at once!"

Moments later, the palace physicians arrived. After much examination and deliberation, they concluded, "Your Highness, the gods have answered our prayers. The queen is with child."

Queen Adélolá burst into tears.

King Àjosè hugged her. "Lolá, I share in your tears of joy. We have awaited this moment for a long time. Let us thank the gods for this pleasant news."

Adélolá's mind reeled. She felt a mix of emotions—happy, sad, confused, guilty—and was unsure of what to do amid the happiness. Her mind was in chaos.

Kúyè sat in his quarters, deliberating how to handle the situation. Moments later, he sent for Lúlù. "Lúlù, I hope you're feeling well."

"Yes, my lord. I hope there is no problem," she answered.

"No problem whatsoever, Lúlù." Kúyè put his hands behind his back. "Go home and spend some time with your family. The queen's order."

"But ... I ... I do not understand, my lord," Lúlù said. "I saw Her Highness yesterday, and she did not tell me to—"

"Well, she told me today," Kúyè interjected.

Lúlù nodded. "Very well, my lord. I shall pack a few things and say goodbye to Her Highness before I—"

"She is in no condition to see anyone now. She fainted earlier today, and she's resting now. The queen shall send for you when the time is right."

"Very well, I shall pack my items and be on my way."

"I shall arrange for some guards to escort you home safely," he said.

"Thank you, my lord." Lúlù left Kúyè's quarters, feeling confused and hurt by the sudden dismissal. She was not allowed to see the queen before she left the palace and headed home.

Days later, Queen Adélolá felt more like herself. She sat in her chamber with some of her maids. "Please, get me Lúlù at once."

"Lúlù left the palace a few days ago, Your Highness."

"Left for where?" she asked.

"For Sàbẹ, Your Highness," the maid replied.

"She left the palace without my consent? Is her mother ill?" the queen asked.

"I am not sure, my queen," the maid replied.

"I believe Elder Kúyè had something to do with her leaving, my queen," another maid piped up.

"Elder Kúyè?" said the queen. "Get me Elder Kúyè at once!"

"Yes, Your Highness." A maid hurried off.

Moments later, Kúyè entered the queen's chamber. "My queen?" He bowed.

The queen turned to the maids. "Leave us."

"Your Highness." The maids stood up and left the queen's chamber.

The queen stared at Kúyè. "Who gave you the audacity to send my maid away?"

"Do not be upset, my queen. It is for the best," Kúyè replied calmly.

"How do you mean?" the queen asked.

"A few days ago, I advised her to go to Sàbẹ. This shall keep her away from the public eye until she gives birth—so that people will not ask questions, my queen."

"And you did not think it was proper to get my approval?"

"Forgive me, my queen. You were a bit under the weather at the time."

The queen was displeased, but felt it might be the right approach to keep Lúlù's pregnancy undisclosed until she birthed her child. "Make sure you keep an eye on her—and make sure she lacks nothing in Sàbẹ."

"Very well, my queen. I shall make sure of it." Kúyè bowed and left the queen's chamber.

A few days later, Kúyè summoned three warriors to the palace.

Àdìgún, Dìran, and Jantaa entered a small private room inside the palace.

"Thank you for honoring my call, great warriors of Odùduwà."

They bowed on one knee.

"It is an honor, my lord."

Àdìgún, Dìran, and Jantaa were skilled warriors. Àdìgún was bearded and lanky. He was cautious in his ways and stronger than he looked. Dìran was tall and strong. He was ruthless and a loyal warrior. Jantaa was short and heavy. He was also strong and loyal to the throne.

Kúyè stated, "By order of the queen, go to the village of Sàbẹ and get rid of Lúlù at once—without any trace. Leaving her alive is a threat to the throne. You shall be greatly rewarded after the mission."

"Very well, my lord. We shall be on our way." They nodded dutifully and headed out.

CHAPTER 5

Betrayal

Lúlù sat in a chair, her eyes downcast. She was lost in her own thoughts, wondering why the queen had sent her away. *Obviously, it was to hide the pregnancy.* But it felt like there was something more. Something ominous. *No, that's not fair. The queen has always been good to me and has treated me with kindness.*

A loud thud stirred a scattering of spices into the air, breaking Lúlù's thoughts as she coughed and swatted the cloud away. "Màmá?"

Móńjé plopped into a chair next to Lúlù and began rummaging through a brown sack. Móńjé was a powerful seer in her own right; she had an oracle's spirit. She was full of wisdom and knowledge. Her garments were always white, which indicated purity, and she wore red beads in her hair and around her neck, wrists, and ankles. She pulled out her *ifá* oracle—a collection of sixteen cowrie shells—and a brown calabash bowl from the sack. The ifá oracles were cowrie shells known to possess godlike powers that were used to consult the gods for clarifications on unclear important matters.

"You are troubled, little fawn," she said gently.

"Tired, Màmá," Lúlù said. "Just tired."

Móńjé thumped her on the head with a spoon. "Your màmá is a seer, yet you lie. Not wise, my child."

Lúlù rubbed her head. "I'm not lying, Màmá." *Just not telling the whole truth.*

Móńjé snatched up the cowrie shells and tossed them in the calabash bowl. She spent some time contemplating their orientation.

Lúlù had seen this a thousand times, but she lacked her mother's gift.

Móńjé raised a brow and opened one eye wide. "Uh-huh. So, you say."

"What is the Odù telling you, Màmá?" Lúlù asked.

"Hmm, the ant that is destroying the kola nut lives inside the kola nut. Ifá is telling me that your queen is expecting." Móńjé said. "Now, tell me, child, what happened?"

Lúlù told Móńjé about her encounter with the king, the pregnancy, and what Kúyè had told her.

"My child, I have seen all of these things before you opened your mouth to say a word. I saw a glimpse of your future before the gods brought you to me. The fearful thing about your journey is that you could walk the path that shall lead you to a good place or take the path that shall lead to a terrible outcome. Unfortunately, I cannot make the choice for you. You have to choose, my child."

"What do I do now, Màmá?" Lúlù was worried and confused.

"Even though your child shall be considered a bastard because you're not married to the king, he will still be the first child from the king's loin. And, according to Odùduwà tradition, he should rightfully be King Àjosè's successor. The queen's child shall be second in line to the throne, and this might displease the queen."

"But the queen has been good to me, Màmá." Tears welled up her eyes.

Móńjé gave a sympathetic glance at Lúlù. "The tides have turned, my child. The rain beats the leopard's skin, but it does not wash out the spots. A woman shall sacrifice all for her child."

"I do not understand, Màmá. The queen does not want to see me anymore?"

"It is not the queen. It is the queen's chief adviser who is the ant inside the kola nut," Mónjé answered.

Lúlù looked at her stomach and rubbed it gently. "And he wants my child?"

"No, not your child. You have to leave and find safety in a far-off land if you want to stay alive long enough to have the child."

Lúlù felt surprised. *Does she want to send me away? Does she think something bad is going to happen?* "Where do I go now, Màmá? How do I survive?"

"I shall send a message to an oracle called Gbàjà in the Dahomey kingdom. I shall use one of my ravens to deliver my message to her before your arrival. She'll know what to do when she gets my message."

"Are you saying I have to leave?" Lúlù asked.

Mónjé looked at the cowrie shells in the calabash bowl and then directly into Lúlù's eyes. "I'm saying *àjà* (hurricane) is always moving and never settles. You must be like àjà for a while, child."

"The Dahomey Empire is far, Màmá," said Lúlù.

"I know, my child. I'm sorry. This is your burden to carry, but you are not alone. The gods and the oracles of our land shall guide you."

Lúlù began to cry.

Mónjé held Lúlù's hand and wiped away the tears with a wrinkled hand. "Do not fret, child. I've seen much. There is a power inside you that you must learn to unleash when the time comes."

"What power, Màmá?" asked Lúlù.

"You shall discover it when the time comes." Mónjé looked at the cowrie shells in the calabash bowl again. "Hmm. Èjì-Ogbè. You are in alignment with destiny, little fawn. Àjà is always moving, clearing any obstacle in its path. So you must be, child. You must hurry now. Danger is fast approaching as we speak. Come, child."

They went inside the hut, and Mónjé prepared Lúlù for the journey.

The warriors were still far off but were getting closer with every step of their horses' hooves. They rode all night toward Mónjé's hut.

Mónjé could see them coming. She started chanting and stirring up a strong wind to slow the three warriors and buy Lúlù some time.

Móńjé saddled her only horse with light clothes, some food, water in a little calabash jar, and preserved fruits that could last Lúlù for the greater part of the journey.

Móńjé blessed her and sent her away.

Lúlù rode off into the dark night.

Móńjé took one of her ravens from a cage, fastened a note between its claws, and released it in the direction of Dahomey.

The raven cawed as it flew away.

CHAPTER 6

Unofficial Assignment

The wind started to howl and blow heavily. Rain soon followed with thunder and lightning.

"The rain is too heavy!" Àdìgún shouted above the wind.

"We cannot even see where we are going!" Dìran exclaimed.

"It is too windy, and the thunder is startling the horses," Jantaa added.

The horses neighed and reared out of control, refusing to move forward because of the wind.

"We shall approach the cave of the dead shortly. We should take shelter there until the storm subsides," said Àdìgún.

The warriors reached the cave, dismounted, and rushed inside with their horses. They found dried sticks and bones in the cave and made a fire. This was the first time since their meeting with Kúyè that they had sat down to ponder their mission.

Àdìgún looked at both men. "My fellow warriors, what do you think about this mission Elder Kúyè has given us?"

"What do you mean?" Dìran asked.

"There's nothing to think about. We carry out the mission and report back to the elder," Jantaa replied flatly.

"Look at the weather. I think this is a warning from the gods to not carry out this mission," Àdìgún said. He looked to the ground and continued. "He who shoots an arrow up in the air and covers his head with a mortar has forgotten that the rest of his body is exposed to the same danger."

The wind howled outside, and the heavy rain continued. Everything outside the cave was barely visible.

Àdìgún continued, "I heard she is pregnant. Think about it well, my fellow warriors. Why Elder Kúyè would want to do this is beyond me. I cannot speak for you, but as for me, I cannot kill a mother and an unborn child. To kill Lúlù shall not go down well with my spirit. When the rain stops, I shall head back."

Dìran could not reason beyond the mission and Kúyè's reward. "The elder said leaving her alive is a threat to the throne, and that is enough reason for me."

Jantaa looked at Dìran and Àdìgún. "I too believe that is a good enough reason to complete this mission."

Àdìgún glanced at both men, trying to read them. "Everyone knows that Lúlù has been nothing but faithful and loyal to the queen. My conscience shall not allow me to carry this out. Besides, I have a pregnant wife at home. I am sorry, my fellow warriors, but I respect your decisions. I shall turn back as soon as the wind calms down."

Dìran stood up and said, "Stop your mouth there, Àdìgún! You think you are better than us, eh? This mission is by the order of the queen, and we all must carry it out or else!"

"Or else what?" Àdìgún shouted.

"We cannot let you leave here alive, Àdìgún." Jantaa slowly got up with Dìran.

Àdìgún jumped to his feet, holding his dagger in his right hand. He was set to attack if need be. "I'd like to see you try!"

"So be it." Jantaa drew his dagger and moved slowly to circle behind Àdìgún.

Dìran lunged forward rapidly and thrust his spear at Àdìgún's chest. It was a predictable opening move that Àdìgún had prepared for. He swiftly turned his right shoulder sideways to avoid Dìran's spear, but the tip of Dìran's spear scraped his flesh. It was painful but not fatal.

Àdìgún continued to rotate in a full circle. He stepped toward Dìran and smashed the tall man's nose with a vicious headbutt.

Dìran fell back, his nose fountaining blood, but Àdìgún had little time to savor the victory.

Jantaa had circled around to Àdìgún's side and thrust a dagger toward his torso. Lightning erupted outside, outlining Jantaa's treacherous form.

With the speed of a panther, Àdìgún spun around and landed a solid kick to Jantaa's stomach. He watched with satisfaction as his opponent crumpled to the ground. The satisfaction was short-lived. A moment later, Dìran's leg snapped out decisively and swept Àdìgún's feet from under him. He crashed to the floor. His eyes filled with stars. Pain erupted inside his head, but there was no time to nurse the pain. He gave Dìran a strong kick to the jaw.

Jantaa moved toward Àdìgún again. Àdìgún stood up with his last ounce of strength. He had to make a hasty decision if he wanted to stay alive.

He held his wounded side as he staggered into the heavy rain, leaving his horse behind.

Dìran was in pain from the kick to his jaw, but he managed to rally with the help of Jantaa. They dashed after Àdìgún on foot, but it was impossible to see more than a few feet ahead in the dark and stormy weather. They lit sticks with fire to search, but the wind blew them out instantly.

"Let him go," Dìran said. "He shall die from the wound—he is on foot."

They wobbled through the darkness and returned to the cave. They needed time to nurse their own wounds.

CHAPTER 7

Lúlù's Background

Twelve full moons before Lúlù's birth, the Odùduwà kingdom had hosted one of their festive gatherings. Òbe was the son of the head blacksmith. He was a dark, handsome, and well-built man from the village of Sàbẹ. One afternoon, he saw a beautiful and shapely girl named Àbèbí, the daughter of a farmer. Their eyes locked, and it was love at first sight.

Òbe approached Àbèbí and said, "*E k'áàsán o* (good afternoon). Are you from here?"

"E k'áàsán o. I'm from the village of Ìlóbù," she replied. "What about you?"

"I am from the village of Sàbẹ," Òbe replied with a flirty smile. "I must say, you look wonderful."

Àbèbí smiled. "È'èhń. Is that why you're boring a hole in my head with your stare?"

Òbe laughed. "How would you have known if you were not looking back, eh?"

Òbe and Àbèbí walked and talked together for the entire festival.

After the festival ended, Òbe would visit Àbèbí. She would make sure she had something refreshing to serve him after the long walk to see her. They enjoyed each other's company and became close; everyone who knew them saw how fond they were of each other.

Òbe was a good blacksmith, and he often helped his father at his workshop to make farming tools and weapons. The knives and spears used by the king's guard were essential for the kingdom. Blacksmiths were renowned for their workmanship, and the profession was a noble one.

Àbèbí often kept Òbe company as he worked the hot coals and furnace. She would sing to him and tell him stories. When Àbèbí was tilling the ground or harvesting crops at her father's farm, Òbe would help her. Most times, he did all the work. At the same time, Àbèbí would sit and entertain him with stories and songs she had learned from her mother.

Many suitors had asked for Àbèbí's hand in marriage, but she had turned them down as many times as they had asked. They became indignant at Àbèbí's refusal to pick her potential husband from her village and tribe. For this reason, a few of them formed a group to disrupt Òbe and Àbèbí's relationship by any means they could.

One fateful day, Òbe's father said, "Òbe, my son!"

"Yes, Bàbá?" he answered.

"I need you to deliver these finished farm tools to our customers. They are overdue."

"Very well, Bàbá," said Òbe respectfully.

"And don't forget to collect the rest of our payment."

"I won't forget, Bàbá." He saddled his horse, loaded the farm tools on his horse, and left.

On his way back, three young men from the village of Ìlóbù approached on horseback.

One of the young men asked, "You are Òbe, àbí (right)?"

"Yes, I am," replied Òbe. He moved closer. "How may I help you?"

"You are trespassing on our territory," said another man.

"I do not understand," replied Òbe.

The third man moved closer. "Òré (friend), we are talking about your relationship with our Àbèbí."

Òbe chuckled. "Is this why you have all come to cross me? Are we all not citizens of Odùduwà? We are one."

"It shall be in your best interest to stop seeing her," said one of the men.

Òbe started to walk away, but then he changed his mind. He turned to the three men. "I shall marry Àbèbí very soon, and there is nothing any of you can do about it."

The men were outraged and drew their daggers.

"We cannot allow that to happen!" yelled one of the men.

Òbe kept his favorite dagger around his waist whenever he ventured far from home. He drew his dagger and took a few steps back, daring the men to approach.

One of the men swung his dagger at Òbe, aiming to cut him deep in his stomach.

Òbe reacted swiftly and moved out of the way. He landed a massive blow to the jaw of the second man as he closed in. The recipient let out a painful shout.

The third man struck a kick that hit Òbe's ribs.

Òbe returned the favor. He spun around and gave the man a vicious kick in his groin. He immediately followed it with a knee to the gut of his first attacker.

Òbe had disoriented all three men within seconds, but in the heat of the moment, he did not notice one of the men had pulled out a sharp dagger. In the moment of distraction, he threw it at Òbe. The dagger pierced his abdomen and stayed lodged. Òbe let out a scream. Everything went silent except for the flutter of wings as startled birds flew away. Òbe felt cold and slowly looked down at his stomach. Blood spilled from his gut. With both hands holding the wound, he collapsed and closed his eyes.

"Ah!" exclaimed one of the men. "Who told you to kill him?"

The man who threw the dagger responded, "I did not mean to. I just wanted to frighten him."

The third man stood up. "What do we do now?"

The killer replied, "We cannot tell anyone about this. Let us pull him to the side and cover him with leaves."

"I do not think that is a good idea," said the third man.

"What then do you suggest?" the killer asked.

"We should throw him in the river. It shall carry him far away from Ìlóbù and protect us from any suspicion," the third man answered.

"Very well. Let us be fast about it before someone sees," the killer responded anxiously.

They threw Òbe's body in the river and headed back to their village. Òbe's body floated away with the current.

Hours turned into days, and Òbe's father grew more and more worried about the prolonged absence of his son.

Àbèbí was also very worried. She had not heard from Òbe, and no one had news of his whereabouts.

The villages of Sàbẹ and Ìlóbù pitied Àbèbí. They sent out search parties; night and day, small groups combed every nook and cranny of the forest, but there was no sign of Òbe.

A few days later, fishermen near the Sawè River found Òbe's body. The current had washed it ashore. They carried Òbe's body to his father in Sàbẹ.

His father was heartbroken, and the whole town mourned.

When Àbèbí heard the news, she fainted. She cried and mourned him longer than anyone else. She vowed that she would never yield to another suitor.

A few weeks after Òbe's death, Àbèbí was on her way to the farm. She threw up, but she did not overthink it. It was probably something she ate. The vomiting became incessant, and it seemed to happen in the mornings. She discovered she was carrying Òbe's child. She had mixed emotions. She felt a strange joy that part of Òbe would still be alive in her, but she was sad that he was no more and that she would be an unwed mother. In the land of Odùduwà, it was taboo for a woman to give birth out of wedlock. It would be disgraceful to her and her family, and the punishment was usually severe. She could be banished from the land or stoned to death, depending on the punishment the gods saw fit.

Àbèbí hid her pregnancy from her old parents for months. She would tie an extra scarf around her stomach, underneath her clothes, to conceal the pregnancy.

One day, in the season of the corn harvest, her mother called to her, "Àbèbí!"

"Yes, Màmá?" she answered.

"Hurry to the farm and harvest a basket of corn before nightfall."

"Very well, Màmá." Àbèbí picked up an empty basket. "I shall be on my way now, Màmá." She headed out the door.

"Very well, do not take too long, my daughter."

Àbèbí got to the farm and harvested a basket of corn. The evening was far spent, and it was getting dark. She turned on her lamp, put the basket on her head, and headed home. Suddenly, she felt a sharp pain around her waist. She crouched in agony. She managed to take a few more steps, but the pain became more severe as the baby started to move. She dropped her basket as the labor pains became unbearable. "Somebody, help me!"

There was nobody around to help.

She dragged herself to a tree and started to push, sweating profusely. She pushed to the point of exhaustion, but the baby was not coming out. Blood and body fluids were everywhere, and Àbèbí trembled from the pain. She grabbed some corn, tore off the husk, and bit hard into the grain, masking her screams as she slowly pushed out a tiny baby girl covered in blood. She had no time to rest. She knew her parents would be worried.

Àbèbí cleaned the baby as best she could, took a scarf from her waist, and wrapped it around the baby. She took the pearl from her wrist and put it around the baby's ankle. She left the child under the tree and picked up her basket of corn in painful silence. She took a few steps forward, turned back, and stared at the baby. She burst into tears and shook her head. Her world closed in as she walked away.

Àbèbí was leaving part of her soul behind—her baby and her memories of Òbe. She could feel his spirit around her, but she could not stop. She was terrified of what would happen if anyone discovered she had conceived out of wedlock. She left her newborn in the forest and prayed to the gods to protect her baby. Even so, the cry of the child haunted her. She would take that to her grave.

Ajalamo, the spirit of the unborn in the land, heard the cries of the mother and child. It emerged from the forest in the form of a woman; this was an exceedingly rare occurrence, but this situation was unique.

Looking at the child, she knew the child possessed unusual abilities. She carried the child and entered the tree under which the baby was born. Ajalamo was able to move at a high speed in the network of trees.

A short while later, Ajalamo emerged from the tree in front of Mónjé's hut. She put her hand on the newborn's head and blessed the child. Ajalamo placed her on Mónjé's doorstep and disappeared.

Mónjé returned home from an outing and found a baby on her front step. The baby was still glowing from the presence of Ajalamo. Mónjé knew what the glow meant: she had prayed for a baby several years ago. She picked up the baby, examined her thoroughly, and noticed the pearl wrapped around her ankle. Mónjé sighed. "Hmm, and you brought your name with you. Little one, you shall be called Lúlù."

She looked up thankfully into the forest and bowed. She took the baby as her own and cared for her. Lúlù grew up to be a fine young lady with wisdom and courage under the tutelage of Mónjé.

All who met Lúlù were struck by her beauty. When she became a teenager, the queen took notice of her when she accompanied Mónjé to the royal courts. The queen had the authority to pick whomever she wanted to be her handmaid. Lúlù was among the young ladies picked that season because of her beauty and wisdom. The queen trusted her, and she became the queen's favorite. Several of the queen's handmaids had come and gone, either to return to their parents after their years of service or to get married, and Lúlù was the only one who had stayed by the queen's side for more than a decade. Her loyalty to the queen was invaluable.

CHAPTER 8

The Journey

Lúlù rode through the forest for days, stopping only periodically to regain her strength. Dahomey was still far away. Darkness was creeping in, and she stopped for the day. The fatigue had reached her bones, and she could barely stay on course.

Lúlù found a cave to set up camp, gathered sticks, and made a fire. She took her sack of water and drank from it. As she placed the sack beside her, she felt a bite on her wrist. She looked down and saw a rattlesnake slithering away. She picked up a big stone and threw it at the snake. The big stone hit the snake's head, smashing it flat. Its body convulsed and then became lifeless. She needed to act fast before the poison traveled to her heart. She found a small piece of cloth and tied it above the bitten area. She cut the site of the bite with her dagger, sucked the poison out, and spit it on the floor. She poured some palm wine on the wound, applied dried pepper, covered it with leaves, and tied it up.

Lúlù started to sweat and shiver, feeling weak from the poison. Her vision blurred, and she became delirious. She crawled on the floor with the little strength she had left, placed her blanket on a smooth stone, and drifted off to sleep. The night was dark and cold, but the fire kept her warm. She started to dream.

Lúlù awoke in a place that looked like paradise. She saw beautiful trees with deep green leaves. The flowers danced in the warm breeze, displaying their colors for whoever cared to notice. A beautiful black horse ran past her. She looked in the direction of the horse and saw a little boy sitting on a beautiful throne. He was wearing a white linen gown and a golden crown. He had a golden scepter in his hand and was smiling at Lúlù. Lúlù smiled back with eyes full of tears.

The love radiating from the boy was palpable. The little boy beckoned to Lúlù. "Come," he said.

She took a few steps forward, and then everything changed. The trees and flowers started to burn. She looked to her right and saw a haggard gray horse running past her. She saw the little boy lying on the floor in front of a dark throne. He was wearing dirty, torn clothes, and he held out his hands. "Help me," he said.

Lúlù was confused. She took a few steps forward to help the boy.

Oshosi, the forest spirit, appeared and directed her gaze to a black crow approaching her. It was big enough to swallow a person whole. Lúlù's heart filled with fear at the sight of the crow. It flapped its wings, ready to pounce on her. She took a few steps back and tripped. She fell backward into a hole. The hole became a wide, dark chasm. She screamed as she plunged down the bottomless pit. The crow chased her down the hole.

The crow caught up to Lúlù as she was falling. It opened its mouth and swallowed her. The huge black beak and the dark pink of the bird's mouth gave way to a dark void.

It seemed like a dream inside a dream. Although the crow had swallowed her, it reappeared in front of her. Lúlù felt a power overtake her body. She was filled with rage and grabbed the crow by the neck.

The crow cawed loudly and grabbed Lúlù's waist with its sharp claws.

She glanced down and saw the claws had become wiry hands. Lúlù's eyes were now beaming light blue with intense fury. She growled and choked the crow until it went limp. Lúlù awoke from the nightmare shouting. The pain from the snakebite had worn off. Her face bore a wild look. Something had permanently changed inside Lúlù.

The first rays of daylight peeked above the clouds. She saddled her horse and headed south toward Dahomey.

She stopped to rest wherever she found water. The horse was near the point of exhaustion. Lúlù got off the horse and led it slowly along the worn forest path until the horse collapsed, refusing to move. Lúlù prodded the horse to a tree that would provide shelter. *If it doesn't get eaten by a wild beast, it may spend the rest of its days foraging in the forest,* she thought.

Lúlù packed a small bag with essentials and left the rest of her belongings and the horse to fate. She continued alone for hours, making little progress. Her forearm started to bleed again. Her legs ached. Fatigue kicked in, but Lúlù continued wobbling through the forest. She hoped to reach a nearby village or settlement before nightfall.

Lúlù had covered quite a distance since the cave, but she felt lost. She didn't notice that every step was moving her closer to Dahomey, the kingdom her mother had sent her to. She looked up as dusk fell. She took a few more steps and collapsed. Everything became a blur, and she drifted into oblivion.

CHAPTER 9

Flood

The rain stopped at the crack of dawn. Dìran and Jantaa were well rested after the nighttime struggle with Àdìgún. They mounted their horses, left Àdìgún's horse in the cave, and rode off toward Sàbẹ. They soon approached Mónjé's hut.

Mónjé knew they were coming. She sat under a tree close to her domain, waiting for them. The oracle's spiritual powers were known to many in the kingdom.

The men hoped to catch her by surprise. Since she was aged, they expected to subdue her and capture Lúlù before she could react. As they approached Mónjé's hut, they saw her from afar. They dismounted their horses and hid behind the bushes.

"What do we do now?" asked Jantaa.

"I'm thinking," replied Dìran.

"Well, think fast because we're running out of time," snapped Jantaa.

"How about *you* come up with a plan instead of relying on me?" Dìran retorted.

The men's nervousness was getting the better of them.

"Is she still sitting there?" asked Dìran.

Jantaa raised his head from behind the bushes. To his surprise, Mónjé was no longer seated under the tree. "I can't see her."

"What do you mean?" Dìran asked.

"Take a look yourself," replied Jantaa.

Dìran raised his head and looked. "She's not there, Jantaa."

Suddenly, Mónjé appeared behind them. She was dressed in an elegant white wrapper with glowing white beads around her head, neck, waist, wrists, and ankles. "To what do I owe this surprise visit, my lords?"

The two men jolted back, but quickly pulled themselves together, trying to hide their nervousness.

"We are here by the order of the queen, my lady," said Dìran.

"Yes, that … that is why we are here, my lady," said Jantaa.

"So why do you have to hide in the bushes to deliver a message from the palace, my lords?"

"We were not hiding, my lady. We were just um … resting," answered Dìran uneasily.

"Follow me, my lords," Mónjé said.

The men walked behind her as she led them to her small hut.

"What can I offer my lords?" Mónjé asked.

"We shall pass, but thank you, my lady. We have a personal message for Lúlù," Dìran replied.

"Ah, for Lúlù? You just missed her, my lords," Mónjé said. "She just left for the palace not too long ago. The queen sent for her."

Dìran and Jantaa were unsure whether Mónjé was trying to mislead them.

Dìran touched the dagger around his waist to intimidate Mónjé, but he did not draw it. "Look, woman! Do not play with us! Tell us where Lúlù is this instant!"

Jantaa stood beside Dìran, also clutching his dagger.

Mónjé realized the men could attack her at any moment. She had no physical strength for battles. She needed time to cast a spell. "I think you should ask the person who sent you where Lúlù is."

Enraged, Dìran pulled out his dagger, moved behind Mónjé, and put his dagger to her throat. "Tell us where Lúlù is, old woman," he whispered menacingly.

She remained quiet.

"Tell us!" shouted Jantaa.

Móńjé looked at Jantaa with a smile. She floated through the dagger and across the room like water. "Save your threats, young man." She turned toward the young warriors.

They looked at each other, a bit confused, but not surprised at Móńjé's abilities. They had been trained to be fearless.

Dìran moved quickly toward Móńjé, and Jantaa circled to strike her from the back.

Móńjé swept her hands in circular motions, sending the young warriors flying backward without physically touching them.

The two warriors hit the wall and crashed to the floor. They tried to regain their bearings. They were not going accept defeat; warriors of Odùduwà never backed down from anything or anyone.

"You little lads can't even discern vegetables from herbs," Móńjé said calmly.

Móńjé raised her hands again, lifting the warriors from the ground with a simple motion of her hands. She gazed intently at them as they hung between heaven and earth.

Jantaa and Dìran struggled in the air.

Dìran managed to pull a bow from his back and an arrow from his sack. He nodded to Jantaa. "Now, Jantaa!"

Jantaa released a black powder into the atmosphere, disarming Móńjé's abilities for a moment. It would not be long before she regained her powers. He quickly released the arrow.

Móńjé wanted to disappear, but she could not. Her powers had been disarmed, and she was defenseless. Her time had come. She looked up and closed her eyes as the arrow pierced her side. Blood gushed out, soaking her white linen.

"Kàkà kí ilè ó kú—ilè á shá," (Instead of the ground's demise—it diminishes in value). Móńjé slowly slipped to the floor. Her powers no longer suspended the men; they fell to the floor with a thud.

"We would not have gotten anything out of her anyway," said Dìran. "The old witch was ready to die."

"She sacrificed her life for Lúlù ... that was noble," Jantaa said quietly. "What do we do now?"

"We must burn down the hut," Dìran replied.

As the men prepared to burn the hut, Móńjé's body turned to water and seeped into the ground. The men stared in shock at the phenomenon and ran from the hut in terror. They stumbled into the forest, falling over trees and shrubs.

Water burst out of the hut, gushing from the point where Móńjé's essence had seeped into the ground. A river formed, sweeping everything in its path. It was headed for the men.

"We should not have killed her!" Jantaa exclaimed.

"We cannot change that now!" Dìran yelled over the sound of the rushing water—in a defeated tone.

The river was not massive, but it was powerful. They had to think fast or be swept away by the current. There was no time to fetch their horses.

"Look over there!" Jantaa pointed to an Ìrókò tree.

The men scrambled up the tree as the water rushed past, drowning the horses. "This is not good, Dìran. Not good at all!" Jantaa shouted.

The two men panted as if they had just run a marathon.

"How do we get back without our horses?" Jantaa said.

"You should worry about your survival first," Dìran said wryly.

After a moment, the river stopped. The water started bubbling in a section close to the tree. A short distance from the men, a form rose from the middle of the river. Still trying to catch their breath, they looked on in shock as the form towered thirty-six feet over the forest floor. Móńjé's spirit embodied the rushing water. She still wore the beads, but they were now large gleaming pearls. She was a beautiful yet frightening sight to behold.

The men looked on in horror as Móńjé said in a low, watery rumble, "Your queen has forced the hands of the gods. She has chosen to be clouded by her own interests and selfishness. She has shed innocent blood. Throughout the reign of Àjosè, the land of Odùduwà shall not see peace for many full moons. The king shall face many calamities. There shall be war from every side. Hardship, injustice, and evil shall consume the land—until the rightful king, chosen by the gods, mounts the throne after Àjosè's reign." The spirit of Móńjé looked at Dìran and Jantaa intently. "As for you two, you have chosen to carry out this evil act. Unlike your fellow warrior, Àdìgún, whom you attempted to kill because he chose the right path, I shall destroy you both. I shall permit you to swim out of my river alive. Nonetheless, you shall not live to see the next festival in the land of Odùduwà. A lad who insults an Ìrókò tree fails to realize that the Ìrókò does not strike back in an instant. I shall allow you to wallow in fear of death until then. As soon as you start to forget your predicament, I shall come for you. The tree remembers what the ax forgets."

The aquatic form collapsed into the stagnant river.

"You both shall die painful deaths—away from the land of your ancestors!" Her voice echoed in the forest.

The river started to flow again.

Jantaa looked at Dìran, terrified. "What have we done?"

Jantaa and Dìran jumped into the river and swam to the other side. Over the course of time, the villagers of Sàbẹ would call the river "the Móńjé River" in honor of the great oracle.

CHAPTER 10

The Queen's Dream

Kúyè sat on a large mat in his quarters, eating and drinking palm wine with his loyal palace maids.

Dìran and Jantaa arrived at the palace, looking disheveled. They requested an audience with the elder.

Kúyè sent the maids away and gestured for the warriors to enter.

They narrated their encounters, but they did not tell the truth about Àdìgún when asked. They simply told him he did not make it.

He gave the men two sacks of silver coins, told them not to tell a soul, and sent them on their way. He anxiously pondered the warriors' accounts, especially of Mónjé's death. News about her disappearance would spread sooner or later. He tried to push it out of his mind and called for his maids to return. "My darlings, please enter!"

Queen Adélolá rested on an expansive, chestnut-brown fur carpet, eating soursop. She felt a strong wind rush into the room, lifting her hair and clothes. It persisted for several seconds, knocking down cups and adornments. The wind let out an ominous howl as it whipped by. She sat up straight. "Did anyone feel that?"

"Feel what, Your Highness?" asked the maids.

She looked around nervously but decided not to be alarmed. "Nothing, I think I'm just tired. I need to sleep. You may all leave."

"Your Highness." The maids left the room.

Queen Adélolá fell into a deep sleep.

She found herself walking in the middle of a thick forest. In the distance, she noticed a small hill. A round stone sat on top of the hill, and the handle of a scepter protruded from it. *What could this mean?* The queen stopped. She could hear children playing in the distance. The phenomenon seemed vaguely familiar.

As she tried to make sense of the scene, the voices got closer. The image became clearer as she moved toward the children. Two little boys were play-fighting with wooden cutlasses. One of the boys was wearing a beautiful white dàshíkí, a sóóró (top and bottom), and fine sandals. The other boy was wearing worn clothes and old sandals. They ran past the queen; they could not see her. She smiled as she watched the boys playing together.

The boys looked up at the hill with the scepter.

Queen Adélolá looked at the boys intently. She was curious to see what they would do with the scepter.

The boys stopped playing and looked at the scepter. It was made of strong brass.

The boy wearing the old sandals raised his wooden cutlass and said, "I am the son of King Àjosè. I am not afraid of anything!"

They both giggled.

The well-dressed boy said, "I, the son of King Àjosè, fear nothing!"

Queen Adélolá's eyes welled up with tears.

The boys were laughing as they ran up the hill.

"Come on," said the boy in the worn clothes.

When they got to the scepter, the boy with the fine clothes looked at the other boy.

"Pull it out," said the boy in the worn clothes.

The well-dressed boy pulled and pulled, but he could not dislodge the scepter. He strained repeatedly and then said, "It's stuck. I can't pull it out. I don't think anyone can."

"Let me try," said the poorly dressed boy.

The first boy stepped aside.

The poorly dressed boy grabbed the golden scepter and pulled it from the stone in one smooth motion.

The scepter lit up, and they both looked surprised.

"How did you do that?" asked the well-dressed boy.

"I don't know," replied the boy in the worn clothes.

Queen Adélolá was confused.

Yemaya, the patron deity of women, rose from the ground and stood beside her.

Adélolá looked to her side, and fell to the ground in shock.

"Do not be afraid, oh queen. I only bring answers to the question you posed in the spirit. You wonder about the boys and why they both claim your husband's name. And why the commoner's son has more ability than the noble-looking one."

Lúlù's picture flashed in the queen's mind. "Lúlù's son?"

"Yes. You cannot force the hand of the gods," Yemaya said.

Queen Adélolá shook her head. "Force the hand of the gods? How? I do not understand."

"Adélolá, let the gods decide the fate of Odùduwà." Yemaya disappeared.

Everything around the queen started to fade, including the two boys with the wooden daggers and the scepter. She could feel the weight of darkness on her skin as her vision ebbed. Queen Adélolá woke up sweating and breathing heavily. She called for her maids, but there was no response.

The palace was silent. Everyone was asleep.

Queen Adélolá's calls echoed into the dead of the night. An eerie silence hung in her chambers as she realized she was alone.

CHAPTER 11

Dahomey

The night sky shimmered. Stars twinkled as the moon rose to its full glory, unabashed as it shed light into dark corners where animals were engaging—and people were seeking privacy. The night air was devoid of the suffocating moisture common to the tropics of Nubia where Dahomey was situated.

The Mino warriors were in the forest tonight for their monthly training. Competitions and training sharpened the skills and wits of the all-female warrior group. The Mino were known for their ferocity; many a man had fallen, assuming that they could easily subdue these females. Queen Témbè had initiated the regiment after many men and resources were lost in battle—to other kingdoms.

Drogba's daughter, Princess Fazilah, oversaw the development of the group. The women had evolved to play a protective and maternal role in the kingdom. The name *Mino* means "our mothers." They were integral to the military and populace; the men provided strength and strategic management, and the Mino handled stealth and special operations.

The Mino were legendary. They sought out females with special abilities and trained the ones who were willing to join. Some were known for being able to see in the dark and long distances, and others could approach without making a sound. Gbàjà, the grand oracle, typically accompanied the warriors and served as a guide during their nocturnal training. Whenever the moon was full and bats blocked the light, it was believed to be a sign of good fortune. Both occurred that night.

The Mino proceeded quietly through the forest.

"The bats are blocking the moonlight," stated Gbàjà. "Tell your warriors to proceed in the direction of the bats."

"Is that where we shall set up camp to train?" asked Ológun, the head of the elite female warrior group. She stood at least a head above the average warrior and had a muscular build. Her smooth, dark sinews glowed in the moonlight.

Gbàjà was aged and wiry. She trembled slightly when she moved, but when she had to, she was capable of speed and strength that belied her age. "We shall see."

The battalion followed the bats a full kilometer through the forest. The moonlight could not penetrate the foliage, so they relied on their instincts to dodge the forest's obstacles.

Gbàjà rode on the back of Beni, her pet baboon.

Beni was Gbàjà's guard and personal assistant. When standing on his feet, Beni was the height of a grown man and had the combined strength of four men. For Beni, carrying Gbàjà was like carrying a child.

The regiment sprang over roots and rocks that jutted out from the ground. Fireflies glowed in the dark, providing sporadic illumination where the full moon could not peer.

The Mino warriors barked and shrieked to create fear in man and animal alike who heard them approach. Predator and prey scurried along the forest floor as the warriors etched a path through the growth. The forest suddenly gave way to a worn path. The warriors emerged from the forest and gathered.

"I don't see anything. Gbàjà, what do you see?" asked Ológun.

The oracle surveyed the path and pointed to the east. "Ojúrí, what do you see?"

"I see a dark object on the path," said Ojúrí.

"Go and bring it," Gbàjà ordered.

"Yes, Mà." Ojúrí rushed off and returned with a bloodstained cloth.

"Ológun, lead in that direction." Gbàjà pointed in the direction where the cloth was found.

Ológun proceeded, and the rest followed.

After several minutes, the group came upon a dark form in the middle of the path.

"It's a woman," said Ojúrí.

Several warriors rushed forward to examine the form.

"Bring her here," Gbàjà requested.

The woman was brought to Gbàjà. She put her ear to the woman's nose. "She is still alive. Bring me the *cakankou*."

A leather pouch with uniquely green leaves was brought to Gbàjà. She put them in a clay pot and crushed them.

The cakankou plant had the natural ability to grow back—even after being pulled from the ground. It was believed to have rejuvenating powers. The oracle opened the woman's mouth and put several drops of the juice from the cakankou leaves on her tongue. She closed her mouth and started to whisper in her ear.

The warriors could barely hear the oracle's muttering.

Gbàjà possessed ancient knowledge that wrought things not possible in the physical.

The woman sat up, gasping for air, and opened her eyes.

The Mino stepped back, alarmed, and drew their weapons.

The woman looked around at the warriors and collapsed again.

Gbàjà put her right hand on the woman's forehead and her left hand on her own forehead. She started chanting again. "Èèwò!" (forbidden) Gbàjà exclaimed. "This is a special woman. She has escaped death several times." She rubbed her hand over the woman's body and stopped at her stomach. Again, she listened to the woman's stomach. "She is pregnant. The spirit of the child speaks to me. The child too has a special destiny."

"This must be the reason for the signs," Ojúrí said.

"Bring more cakankou!" Gbàjà ground some more leaves, added some dark fluid to make the juice known as *àgbo* (herb), and put more drops in the woman's mouth.

The Mino watched the operation in amazement.

Gbàjà started to whisper in the woman's ear again.

The woman sat up violently a second time, but slumped over again.

"Give her some more," Ológun said.

Gbàjà put drops in the woman's mouth a third time and chanted in the woman's ear. "Hit her on her chest," Gbàjà instructed Ológun.

The mighty warrior landed a heavy blow between the woman's breasts.

She sat up, screaming in pain. She stared in confusion at the female warriors surrounding her.

"It is okay, my child," Gbàjà soothed and then turned to Ológun. "Bring me some water."

The woman was given water and a few minutes to come to full awareness.

"Where are you from?" Gbàjà asked.

The woman kept silent.

"Where are you going?" Gbàjà asked.

The woman burst into tears.

Gbàjà cradled the woman in her arms. "There, there. What is your name, my child?"

"Lúlù," she responded through tears.

Gbàjà's eyes lit up. She knew who she was. "Do not fear, child. You are in the kingdom of Dahomey. You shall detail your journey at a later time. We shall take you to meet our king."

"Why do you want to take her to the king?" asked Ológun. Ológun was one of Dahomey's strongest and fiercest warriors. She had a defiant way about her. "I know you want to help this stranger according to our tradition, but you do not know who she is and what she is about."

"I have told you—this one is special. She must meet the king," Gbàjà answered resolutely.

"As you wish," Ológun conceded in exasperation.

The journey to the palace took forever in Lúlù's eyes. She lay in a hammock tied to a stick at both ends. Two female warriors of equal height carried the front and back. Lúlù was still in pain and not in full control of herself.

Gbàjà and her warriors reached the palace and asked the guards to summon the king. The Dahomey palace was massive, and the wall around the palace was as high as the tall trees that surrounded it. Equally tall gates made of wrought iron guarded the palace entrance.

The king emerged from the palace, still half asleep, and took his place on the throne. The warriors stood facing the throne with the stranger.

Gbàjà approached the throne and bowed. "My king, we found this lady in the forest on our training expedition. We saw the sign of the full moon, and the bats led us to her. My king, this woman is someone special. I have had a revelation from the oracles. She has yet to tell her story due to what she has been through, but in accordance with our tradition of hosting strangers, I made the decision to bring her here."

"You do not know who she is?" asked the king, furrowing his brow.

"No, my king," Gbàjà answered. She had received the message from Mónjé's raven before Lúlù's arrival, but the gods had not yet led her to disclose Lúlù's identity.

"And you brought her to my presence?!" the king stormed.

"My king, we should hear her story. The oracles cannot be wrong about her. I did not make this decision surreptitiously," Gbàjà said.

Lúlù was fully conscious now, but she seemed lost as she stared into the distance. She sat on the court floor, rocking slightly back and forth with no expression on her face.

King Drogba looked at Lúlù. "Speak. Who are you, and where are you from?"

She stared at the king blankly. She did not care to speak or engage the king. He could do whatever he wanted. Things could not get any worse.

King Drogba's wife strode into the court. Queen Témbè was short and plump. She exuded a strong motherly aura and commanded respect. She never hesitated to get involved with her subjects. Be it to help with birth and childcare, clean, cook, or provide advice, she was considered the mother of mothers. The queen turned to the king. "Can you not see that she has been through a great ordeal? Allow her to rest and get cleaned up in the guest chambers. Give her food and tend to her wounds. Then you may continue your interrogation." She stared at the king and then at Gbàjà. "Do you know her people?"

"No, my queen," Gbàjà replied.

"Do you know where she is from?" the queen asked.

"The message from the gods is that she is someone to be reckoned with, but that is as far as I know for now, my queen."

The queen said, "There is no rush then. Give her three days, and then bring her back to determine her origins. As long as she is in good health, all else can be resolved."

King Drogba nodded in silent resolution. He knew the mood the queen was in. She felt like she had a duty to save the world. He shook his head.

The queen ignored the king's exasperation and called on two maids. "Lawe, Kinti, follow me. The white lioness is about to deliver. I want to ensure the delivery is safe."

"Your Highness." The maids quickly followed behind, trying to keep up with the queen as she stomped out of the courts.

CHAPTER 12

A New Beginning

Queen Témbè's lions were important in the Dahomey kingdom. She was from the east, where lions roamed the great savannahs. Her father, King Barrack of Abyssinia, had given her a male and a female cub. Dahomey obeyed the rule of seven, and consequently, she was not allowed to have more than seven lions. Presently, she had five. The male was black, the female was white, and their three cubs were golden. The three cubs did not carry the recessive mutation that had caused their parents to be black and white. Témbè was eager to see if the white lioness would produce any more mutated offspring.

Lúlù took the first day to rest and reflect on what had transpired. She thought about her mother and burst into tears. She feared the worst. The warriors going to Mónjé's house was not a good sign. The journey through the forest. The snakebite. The dream. It was all too much in such a short time.

Not so long ago, she had served in King Àjosè's court with the beautiful and benevolent Queen Adélolá. She would have given her life for the queen, but she had turned on her. *After I did everything the queen wanted, I'm no longer needed—now that she has conceived. It was easier for Her Highness to dispose of me and my baby—the heir to the throne—than to risk exposing her selfish act.* Lúlù looked down and rubbed her stomach. "Nothing shall happen to you. I promise. I shall die before I let anything happen to you."

Ológun and Gbàjà sat in the outer courts of the palace, working with the administrators to plan the census. Every ten years, a census was conducted of the Dahomey kingdom to gather demographics. Queen Témbè had brought this tradition from Abyssinia. It had yielded great benefit for her father, and she brought it to Dahomey to help manage the kingdom, especially in the face of attacks that had depleted the population.

Gbàjà looked over a map with two of the administrators. "According to the oracles, we should divide the kingdom into four quadrants and divide the commission into four groups, one to handle each section. Before we do that, it may be beneficial to hear the testimony of our visitor. Her story shall be crucial to future events in the kingdom."

Ológun crossed her arms. "We typically start from the center and move in concentric circles. Now you need the testimony of a stranger to give us permission to conduct a census? I hope you are sure about this."

"You dare question the gods? The gods are never wrong!" Gbàjà scolded.

"I did not see the gods show up in our many battles. When we lost our men, women, and children. Didn't your other oracles get killed in those battles?" Ológun stared down at Gbàjà.

"You have little wisdom. You cannot see further than your nose and physical strength." Gbàjà shook her head.

"I can see whatever I want to see. If I did not lead the army as I did, this kingdom—and maybe even you—would not exist," Ológun said.

"Your physical strength shall not last forever. Do not ever forget that. We shall hear her story, and then we shall know where we stand." Gbàjà turned to one of the administrators. "Bring me the agricultural map. Let us divide the areas for the census."

"The lioness gave birth to three cubs!" Queen Témbè exclaimed as she entered King Drogba's chambers. "Two golden females and one black male!"

"What shall you do with them?" King Drogba asked. "You know the rules. You cannot have more than seven—it may bring a curse. We have had enough trouble in this kingdom."

"My king, if you saw the cubs, it would break your heart to lose any of them," the queen replied. "I have stood by you all these years. I will not bring you any issues."

King Drogba did not always admit it, but Queen Témbè had protected the kingdom of Dahomey from an onslaught of military and economic attacks. She had established the Mino and implemented traditions and norms from Abyssinia.

"Have you spoken to our lady guest? It has been three days," the queen inquired.

"I plan to summon her this evening," King Drogba replied.

Queen Témbè smiled. The king could be quite forgetful. He needed her by his side.

After supper that evening, the king called to the guards, "Bring the guest."

The guards brought Lúlù to the court.

The king and queen sat with their trusted adviser, Bira. Gbàjà and Ológun were also notified of the summons, but Gbàjà did not attend. She had gone into the forest with her baboon, Beni, to replenish her stock of medicinal herbs.

Lúlù nervously walked into the court. She wore a green and yellow wrapper that reached her feet and a matching headwrap. This attire was common in Dahomey. She looked starkly different from the woman they found a few days ago. She was beautiful and shapely, and she carried an aura of importance.

The king nodded to Bira.

Bira was a bald man with a long white beard. He had seen many things he could not utter. He had served Drogba's father and had trained under the adviser to Drogba's grandfather. He was respected by all. "Good evening to you, young lady. We trust you have found these few days in the kingdom pleasant. We seek to know who you are and what journey led to the events in the forest. Different stories have been assumed, but we wish to hear directly from you." He looked intently at Lúlù and spoke with his hands behind his back. He was not one for frivolities.

Lúlù knelt to greet everyone with respect, which was common in Odùduwà and the surrounding kingdoms. "Your Highnesses and elders, I greet you and thank you from the bottom of my heart for your accommodation and hospitality. My name is Lúlù, and I am from the Odùduwà kingdom."

A few gasps were heard in the room.

"I never knew my parents. My mother was from Ìlóbù, and my father from Sàbẹ̀, as I was told. They met at a festival and fell in love. My father was killed by some of my mother's suitors from Odùduwà. They were jealous of their relationship."

"How sad," the queen remarked quietly. She leaned in closer. "Please continue, my dear."

Lúlù sighed. "My mother discovered she was pregnant after the death of my father. As you are aware, this is taboo in the land. With my father deceased, my mother had no one to stand for her. She gave birth to me in the forest. Ajalamo, the spirit of the unborn, took me to my adoptive mother, Mónjé." Lúlù went on to describe the events in the palace with Queen Adélolá and King Àjosè and how she had to flee Sàbẹ̀. The events in the forest led to her being discovered unconscious. Lúlù stopped and glanced furtively around the room.

Queen Témbè nodded to her in encouragement.

"I gave my life for my queen, and now I am pregnant with the heir to the throne of Odùduwà. Elder Kúyè, the queen's chief adviser, is after my life since the queen is now carrying her own child. If he finds me, he may kill me." Lúlù bowed her head.

The attendees stared and waited for more, but silence hung in the air.

Bira looked around the court. Those present were visibly moved. Bira turned to Lúlù. "Thank you, Lúlù, for sharing this with the court." He looked to the king. "My king, do you wish to—"

"I am sorry, my lord," interrupted Lúlù. "Where may I find the oracle named Gbàjà? My mother said she shall know what to do when I meet her."

King Drogba stared at her in disbelief.

"Gbàjà, the oracle?"

Lúlù was startled by the king's reaction. She thought she had said something wrong.

The king composed himself and addressed the court, "Silence, everyone. This story remains in the court. Lúlù, you may leave. Thank you."

Lúlù thanked everyone, and the guards escorted her to her quarters.

"Call a meeting for the high chiefs tomorrow." The king turned to Ológun. "Call for Gbàjà at once." He walked outside.

"My king." Ológun acknowledged as she walked out.

One of the elders, Múrí—who had treacherous ways about him and would mostly act if a situation was beneficial to him—slunk away from the crowd, displeased with Lúlù's advent to Dahomey. *There must be some reward given to whoever finds her. Besides, she may bring unwarranted troubles to our shore,* he thought as he walked away. Múrí reached his hut, took one of his ravens, fastened a note to its claws, and sent it in the direction of Odùduwà.

CHAPTER 13

Fate of a Stranger

King Drogba paced back and forth, slowly counting his steps. "We have a problem." He looked up, holding his hands behind his back. "A problem of epic proportions."

This time, only the king's closest advisers, chiefs, and elders were present, as well as the queen. Moments later, Gbàjà and Ológun entered the court and stood in front of the king and his committee.

The elders stared at the oracle and the warrior through their dim black eyes and white beards.

"Gbàjà, you thought this was a good idea? I should have your head for this!" The king glared at the oracle. "And you, Ológun, you stood by and let this happen. You are the premier guard of the kingdom. Unbelievable!"

"My king, I advised against it, but my advice fell on deaf ears." Ológun pointed to Gbàjà.

"My king, I would never do anything to jeopardize the kingdom. I merely followed the instructions of the gods," Gbàjà explained.

"The gods? The gods told you to bring the enemy into our camp and lie about it?" the king exclaimed. "I shall decide what to do with you … or … perhaps I should have your head for this."

Bira stepped between Gbàjà and the king. He knelt on his right knee, propping up his left elbow on his left knee. This posture showed utmost respect for the king. "My king, if I may speak?"

"You may, Bira," King Drogba answered.

"Gbàjà has been a trusted spiritual adviser. She has the good of the kingdom at heart. If I may be allowed to plead her cause: her head should remain on her body for the rest of her life, and definitely tonight."

The chiefs and elders grunted in agreement.

Gbàjà gave Bira a look of thanks.

Bira continued, "She acted according to the bidding of the gods. As such, we must seek to understand what the gods are saying. This lady, Lúlù, is from Odùduwà. Yes, they have attacked us in the past, but she is not an ally of the crown now. If her story is true, she is now an enemy of the royal family, or at least Queen Adélolá. There may be something beneficial in all of this."

King Drogba contemplated Bira's words. "But she said she carries the successor to the throne. The best thing would be to kill her and the unborn child and reduce the possibility of future conflict for ourselves."

"My king, may we speak for a moment?" requested Queen Témbè.

The king glared at the queen. The court fell silent. This was a personal moment between the king and the queen. King Drogba had been known for his temper as a young man, and it sprang up every now and then. Only the queen could calm him down. Many people pleaded their cases to the queen because it was often difficult to reason with the king.

"We shall meet again in one hour. If I do not resolve this matter tonight, someone shall have their head on a stake!"

Everyone bowed in unison and left the room. "Káááabíèsí o!"

Once the king and queen were alone, King Drogba said, "Témbè, I am not in support of you interrupting my meetings with the chiefs. This is a matter of security. You oversee the Mino with your daughter. The men do not interfere with that. Now we seek to find a solution to a situation as crucial as this, and I get interrupted." The king breathed heavily in agitation.

The queen nodded in acknowledgment. "My king, you are my head and ruler, and I shall not go against you. You are also my husband, and

I only seek what is best for you, myself, and the kingdom. Please do not take offense at my interruption. Our tradition dictates that we do not afflict a stranger in our midst, especially one in time of need. To say you shall kill Lúlù and her unborn child is an abomination."

The king responded, "Do you want to fight off the Odùduwà kingdom yourself?"

Queen Témbè looked directly into King Drogba's eyes. "I have fought before, and I shall fight for my king again. You are aware of my lineage. That is part of why you asked for my hand in marriage."

The wind blew softly through the trees, and the leaves rustled as if to validate the queen.

Drogba gazed at her in quiet agreement. He knew he would not win this argument.

The queen continued, "My humble opinion is that we should aid her in any way possible to help her find her purpose. She can leave if or when she decides, but she is welcome to stay if she wishes. We shall keep a close watch over her. She is not a threat; she is in need."

"What if she returns to Odùduwà and exposes our secrets, and they come to annihilate us?"

"Trust me, my king. I am a woman. If there is one thing I know, a woman will do anything to protect her children. She and the queen are both carrying heirs to the throne. If she were to return to Odùduwà, her enemies would kill her before she exposed any secrets. Whoever desires to destroy Lúlù shall not stop—her child is a threat to the Odùduwà throne."

King Drogba pondered the queen's words. "Témbè, you know I love you, and I listen to your advice, but this? Are you telling me to let her stay?"

"Yes, my king," Témbè smiled.

"And have her baby here?" King Drogba asked.

"Yes, my king," Queen Témbè calmly replied.

"The heir to the throne of Odùduwà, our enemy?" asked Drogba.

"That is exactly what I am saying, my king," the queen answered a third time.

Drogba stared long and hard at the queen. "You shall be the death of me. As you wish. We shall let her stay."

"My king." Témbè knelt and smiled at the king.

He took her hand and raised her up. "I hope we are doing the right thing."

An hour later, the court reconvened. The advisers, chiefs, and elders shuffled across the intricately chiseled and polished granite floor. The queen was always particular about maintaining the floor's luster. Dahomey had maintained trade with the Zulu kingdom for several generations and was grateful for their gift of exotic stones.

The king's guard and some members of the Mino were present. The tension in the air was palpable.

Gbàjà moved gingerly to a corner.

King Drogba stood close to the edge of the court. "I welcome you back to this important gathering. First, let me thank you for your loyalty to the kingdom and the roles you have each played in sustaining the kingdom. We seek to clarify the issue of the lady in our midst, Lúlù, and what to do with her. As you are aware, we have not had the most benevolent relationship with the Odùduwà kingdom. This is unfortunate, but it was not always like this. We were once allies. The identity of the lady in question is no more a secret. What she carries and the possibilities it portends are of great significance to our kingdom. Gbàjà, Ológun, step forward."

Ológun walked to the middle of the court, and Gbàjà followed.

The king looked at Gbàjà and Ológun. "I have decided to keep the lady in the kingdom as a guest and observe her for a time. She is pregnant, and she shall remain here until her delivery. We may revisit the issue after this time. Thank you for your service and loyalty, Gbàjà and Ológun." The king looked at Gbàjà and smiled. "You shall keep your head. You and Ológun brought her here, so you two shall be responsible for her. Thank you all." King Drogba strode resolutely out of the court with his hands behind his back.

Queen Témbè paused for a second and smiled at everyone as she followed King Drogba to his chambers.

Members of the audience smiled back and nodded in appreciation. They could always count on her to be an advocate.

CHAPTER 14

Glow

Kúyè sat in his chamber, eating groundnuts and drinking palm wine with his loyal maids, when a raven landed on his window. He took the note from its claws. His eyes lit up as he read the note. *Hmm, so this is where you are hiding. Yes, Elder Múrí, you shall be greatly rewarded.* He dismissed the maids and sent for Jantaa and Dìran.

At sundown, Jantaa and Dìran entered the palace through a back door to avoid being seen. They bowed. "My lord, you sent for us?"

"Yes. I have news of Lúlù's whereabouts," Kúyè stated. "She has taken refuge in Dahomey. Go at once and finish the job quietly. Shut her up for good."

Jantaa and Dìran bowed again. "Very well, my lord."

Lúlù awoke from a deep sleep. It was dawn, the day after the meeting of the elders. She knew she had been on the agenda, but that was all. Lúlù thought of the king's reaction when she had asked for Gbàjà. She could not make sense of it. As far as she knew, she was a guest in the kingdom and had been treated hospitably.

Lúlù heard shrieks outside and the scuffle of feet.

Lúlù sat up to listen.

Someone barked, "Lúlù, come out at once!"

It sounds like Ológun. Lúlù dressed quickly and stepped out of her hut to see the Mino sparring in their training gear. *Are they always training?*

"Do you know how to fight?" Ológun asked.

"I've not had much need for that," Lúlù said.

"Well, you shall need that here. You shall train with us this morning. I shall test you over the next two weeks to see if you have the capacity to join the Mino."

"I'm not sure I am interested in joining the group. I don't think I am a warrior like you women—"

"You have no choice in the matter. To survive here, you must train," Ológun said.

Ológun instructed the women to form a circle and paired several women to fight with sticks.

After a few minutes, Ológun turned to one of the warriors. "Give her a stick, Ojúrí. You two shall fight."

Ojúrí smiled coyly and handed Lúlù a long stick. Ojúrí seemed to walk on her toes, ready to defend herself at a moment's notice.

Lúlù felt very uncomfortable.

Ojúrí crouched and stared at Lúlù. "Move!" She lunged at Lúlù with her stick.

Lúlù blocked it.

Ojúrí swung and hit her arm. "You are slow. Move!" She lunged again.

Lúlù tried to block the stick, but it hit her chest. *That hurt.* Lúlù was irritated. The strikes were painful. She had been in the royal courts for most of her life. *All this fighting is not for me.*

Ojúrí slapped her hand, which stung. She cracked the stick on Lúlù's right shin, sending her to the ground with an eruption of pain.

Lúlù was now angry. She gritted her teeth, scooped up a handful of dirt, and threw it down in a cloud. She rose to her feet, stick held in front, and growled, "Try that again."

Ojúrí grinned and made another charge at Lúlù, targeting her stomach this time.

Lúlù's world slowed down. She felt like she was watching herself and thinking a few seconds before things happened. She seemed to have some control of time. She saw the stick coming. Her only thought was of her baby. *Nothing will ever harm my baby!* She swung the stick counterclockwise, shattering Ojúrí's stick and hitting her in the head. With the same force, she knocked her to the ground. Lúlù jumped into the air, turning a full circle with her stick. She landed with a foot on either side of the warrior, about to strike again.

Ojúrí stared up at Lúlù in disbelief. The morning sun disappeared as she lost consciousness.

The training came to a halt.

"Enough!" Ológun yelled.

Lúlù's eyes glowed dull blue as she glared at Ojúrí, still holding the stick in her hand.

Gbàjà started clapping, and Beni the baboon joined in. "Oo o o ah ah ah!" he barked.

The glow faded from Lúlù's eyes.

"Impressive." Ológun took the stick from Lúlù. "Very impressive. I thought you said you didn't know how to fight."

"I ... I ..."

The Mino carried Ojúrí away.

"Don't worry. She'll be fine," Ológun said. "Let's move on to another exercise. We shall test your strength."

The warriors moved to another part of the training ground. One of the Mino climbed onto a two-foot rock slab and was handed two metal buckets filled with stones. The warrior squatted up and down while holding the buckets.

The other warriors counted and cheered.

The first warrior reached fifteen. The next got to eighteen.

"Lúlù, your turn," Ológun said.

The crowd went silent.

Lúlù picked up the buckets and started.

"One. Two."

She got to nine, and to everyone's surprise, she kept going. It was hard for Lúlù to explain. She was under extreme duress, but she could handle it—she was even starting to enjoy the training.

"Fifteen."

She was shaking.

"Sixteen."

Ológun stood in front of Lúlù, her face a mere six inches from Lúlù's as she came down on the next squat.

"Seventeen."

Lúlù let out a shriek.

The warriors shouted, "Eighteen!"

"Keep going! Up!" Ológun screamed.

Lúlù's entire frame shook from the pressure. She let out another scream.

"Nineteen!"

Lúlù's legs trembled as she came down. She was about to drop the bucket.

"Don't drop it, Lúlù!" Ológun hissed. "Give me one more."

Their noses almost touched.

Lúlù heard a voice in her head. *You can do it.* She growled and shook as she rose for the twentieth time.

The warriors stared in admiration.

Lúlù straightened up under the pressure. "Twenty!" Lúlù shouted and let go of the buckets. She raised her hands to her face and stared at them. Her palms were glowing bright blue.

Gbàjà and Lúlù sat with their legs crossed in Gbàjà's hut.

"You have exceptional abilities. Why have you kept them a secret?" Gbàjà queried. Her ifá cowrie shells were strewn across the mat in the center of the hut. This was where she performed her consultations and received messages from the spirit realm.

Ológun stood with her hands on her hips, watching quietly.

Beni stood behind Gbàjà, seemingly intrigued by what was going on.

Lúlù still felt dazed from the morning's events. "I am truly unaware of these abilities. All I can say is that my adoptive mother, Mónjé, told me I had gifts—and that when the time was right, I would discover them."

"Móńjé? She was an exceptional oracle." Gbàjà paused. "So, what is right about this time, my child? Why are these powers manifesting?"

Lúlù said, "I do not know. This morning, I heard a voice inside speaking to me."

"A voice in your head?" asked Ológun.

"Yes, the voice sounded like that of a child. I think it is the voice of my child," Lúlù replied.

"And this started when you were training this morning?" Ológun asked.

"Yes," confirmed Lúlù.

"Very well then," Gbàjà said. "You shall journey into the spirit realm to learn who is speaking to you. We shall reconvene tonight at the first glimpse of moonlight."

Lúlù did not feel ready for this journey, but she tacitly agreed. She was desperate to understand her newfound powers.

CHAPTER 15

Assimilation

Queen Témbè strode into the den that housed the lions. A stale smell hung in the air. Her white lioness, Mimi, was caring for her new cubs. They had urinated in the straw where Mimi slept. All three cubs were struggling to nurse.

The lioness let out a quiet rumble when she saw the queen. Queen Témbè had cared for her since she was a cub. Mimi was fiercely loyal and protective of the queen.

"Hello, Mimi. How are you, my dear?" The queen rubbed the lioness's head.

Mimi purred again.

The lion in the adjoining den roared. Kabu, the male, stuck his head through an opening and roared again.

"Kabu!" she exclaimed fondly.

Kabu was black from head to toe. He was a majestic and powerful beast.

The queen rubbed his head and then rubbed her face against his. She remembered when he was just a cub. Now he was huge and looked scary, but to her, he would always be little Kabu.

He licked her cheek all the way to her head and knocked off her crown.

"Uh-oh." Témbè gasped.

A small cub in the straw was struggling to breathe. The crown had encircled the cub. Its black color contrasted with the red beads of the crown.

"Who do we have here? Another Kabu? You are black like your father. We shall call you Papu." The queen held up the cub. Mucus was blocking his nose.

Mimi brushed off the two other cubs and approached Témbè. She trusted the queen with her cubs and would give her life to protect the queen. She saw Témbè as a mother.

The queen put her mouth over the cub's nose, sucked out the mucus, and spat it on the straw. She did this several times until the cub was able to breathe again. She put Papu down, and Mimi licked the queen to express her thanks.

The guards who were waiting on the queen looked on in amusement.

Queen Témbè's dress was strewn with straws as she tended to the cubs. She truly was the mother of mothers in Dahomey. "Now that is done," she said matter-of-factly. She picked up the other cubs and examined them. They were female. She named the lighter one Riro and the darker one Princess. She smiled to herself. *Look at my lions.* They were one of her few reminders of home. Lions roamed the ranges in Abyssinia. Many members of the upper society had lions as pets and guards, despite the risk they posed to their masters. If they were not properly fed and cared for, they could turn on their owners or handlers. That was part of the intrigue.

Queen Témbè had appointed a caretaker to tend to the lions, but she cared for many of their needs herself. She walked to the opposite wall, peered through the opening, and saw three other white lions. The male was already growing a mane. The two females carried the recessive gene of their mother and retained the white pigment.

White lions were rare. That was why Queen Témbè's father, King Barrack, had selected Kabu and Mimi for her. The other three lions were Mimi's offspring, but they were separated from the newborns to keep them safe. The three lions were now in their adolescence and were too busy fighting to notice the queen.

Princess Fazilah entered the den. "Mother?"

"My daughter!" The queen rushed over to hug Princess Fazilah. "How are your studies in Timbuktu? What did you learn this time?"

"Oh, Mother, it was remarkable. I have many things to tell you," Princess Fazilah responded.

The princess had been studying philosophy and trade at the famous Sankore University in the Songhai Empire. The Tuaregs of Northern Africa had established the city of Timbuktu and developed trade routes that linked North and West Africa.

Queen Témbè and her daughter walked out of the lions' den, and the guards closed the door behind them.

There would be much excitement now that the princess had arrived.

"The clerics of Sankore are renowned. One cleric I met, Ahmed, is so intelligent, Mother. He taught me things that I must share with you."

"We shall talk, my darling. Get cleaned up and rest—and let me clean up too. We shall have a banquet to celebrate your return."

Princess Fazilah ran into Ológun on her way to her chambers.

"Your Highness, welcome back," Ológun said as she bowed.

"Stop with all the formalities. You know I don't care much for it." Princess Fazilah rolled her eyes. "What has been happening with the Mino? I cannot wait to train with them again and teach the warriors everything I've learned."

"You shall find them intriguing, trust me." Ológun said.

"Why do you look so troubled?" Princess Fazilah asked.

"Princess, many things have happened in your absence. You may find them hard to believe," Ológun responded.

"Try me," Princess Fazilah pressed.

"It shall take a long time," replied Ológun.

"Let us go to my chambers," Princess Fazilah responded.

Ológun enlightened the princess about Lúlù and all that had happened since her arrival. Ológun told Fazilah about the connection to Odùduwà and the powers that Lúlù possessed.

After an hour of updates, the princess said, "Take me to meet this woman."

"As you wish, Princess," Ológun responded.

Ológun took the princess to Lúlù's hut, but she was not there.

The neighbors said she had gone to the market.

"Let's go to the market," said Princess Fazilah.

Ológun was surprised. *She is so intent on meeting this woman.*

The duo finally came across Lúlù in the market.

Fazilah watched as Lúlù went from one stall to the next. She chatted jovially with the market women and helped them move their kids out of the way. "She reminds me of Mother. They have similar ways about them."

Fazilah and Ológun went up to Lúlù. The women in the market recognized the princess and greeted her.

"*E k'áásán o, omo-bìrin oba,*" (Good afternoon, Princess). They knelt as a sign of respect.

"*E k'áásán o, èyin ìyáà mi, Báwo l'ojà?* (Good afternoon, my mothers. How are market trades?)

"*Ajé ńwọgbá o, e sé Mà.*" (Trades are going well, thank you, Mà.)

The exchange of pleasantries and greetings was common in Dahomey, just as in Odùduwà. Although the kingdoms were at odds, they shared the same Yorùbá culture. In essence, they were members of the same culture and family.

Lúlù had never met the princess and was amused at the people's reactions toward this woman who everyone was eager to greet.

Ológun signaled to Lúlù to greet the princess.

Lúlù knelt. "Your Highness."

Lúlù and Princess Fazilah's interaction caught the attention of the market people around them.

"Please, get up." Princess Fazilah pulled Lúlù up. "I have heard so much about you. You are quite the woman, I must say."

"I have seen evidence of you in the Mino. I heard that you established the group," responded Lúlù.

Princess Fazilah turned to Ológun. "I like her. Please ensure she attends the welcoming banquet tonight. Please see that she gets whatever she needs."

Princess Fazilah turned back to Lúlù. "I look forward to seeing you there." Princess Fazilah hurried off to her chambers.

"Interesting, the princess has taken an instant liking to you." Ológun smiled. "I shall have clothes for the banquet sent to your room. Is there anything else you need?"

"No, but thank you," Lúlù replied respectfully.

Jantaa and Dìran were among the onlookers. They had blended with the commoners in the marketplace.

"How do we get her now?" Jantaa whispered.

"We shall keep a close watch till she is by herself," said Dìran.

They tailed behind Ológun and Lúlù unnoticed.

Ológun walked slowly to her quarters. She felt a twinge of jealousy as she thought of Lúlù and the attention she had garnered in such a short time. *It seems as if Lúlù is stealing everybody's hearts.*

CHAPTER 16

Into the Deep

The banquet for Princess Fazilah was lavish. The royal table sat twenty people, nine on each side with the king and queen at the ends of the table. The celebration included chiefs, advisers, and immediate and extended family members.

Princess Fazilah sat adjacent to the queen's seat, and Lúlù sat to the left of the princess.

The guard stamped his staff on the ground three times and announced, "Arise for His Highness, King Drogba, and Her Highness, Queen Témbè."

The king and queen wore colorful wrappers and beads that appeared to sparkle as the light fell on them.

"Please be seated," King Drogba stated.

Princess Fazilah leaned over and whispered to Lúlù, "My father is about to tell a story of how great the kingdom was when he was a boy."

The queen sat down, but the king remained standing and addressed the audience.

"Members of the royal family and my distinguished guests, we are gathered tonight to celebrate the return of our daughter, Princess Fazilah. She has spent months in Timbuktu. She will share knowledge that shall advance the kingdom. When I was a mere child, in the days of my father's father …" The king began to recount the great exploits of the men of Dahomey in the days of old. The king was a good storyteller.

The guests listened all night and enjoyed the food and drink. As the banquet came to an end, the king bade the guests good night. As he rose, each guest followed suit to show respect. "It has been a wonderful evening. I shall take my leave now, but may you continue to enjoy the food and drink. My daughter, welcome back." The king started toward the exit.

The queen stood up and leaned between Princess Fazilah and Lúlù. "I hear you are meeting with Gbàjà tonight."

"Yes, Your Highness," Lúlù responded.

"We shall see you there." The queen touched Lúlù's arm and followed the king.

Lúlù looked surprised.

Princess Fazilah noticed the look on her face. "Mother is aware of most things in the kingdom. She wants to help you."

"Your family has been so kind. Thank you for all you have done," responded Lúlù.

The princess smiled. "We shall see you tonight."

At the first glimpse of moonlight, Lúlù, Ológun, Ojúrí, Queen Témbè, and Princess Fazilah gathered at Gbàjà's hut. As usual, Beni the baboon stood quietly behind the oracle.

Gbàjà acknowledged each attendee with a nod. "Thank you for gathering here. Thank you, my queen, and thank you, Princess. The first time I met this young lady, Lúlù, I saw that she has a great destiny. We have seen her training with the Mino. She has special powers that manifest under unique circumstances. She hears a voice that prompts her. Tonight, she shall enter the spirit world to learn who is speaking to her and why. We want to know who and what we have in our hands." She looked at Lúlù kindly. "Are you ready for this journey?"

Lúlù took a deep breath. "I think so," she replied.

"You cannot think so—you must be certain. You must be confident. You cannot afford to make mistakes in the spirit world. It is a timeless realm. If you doubt, what may befall you can be perilous and permanent. You must have a clear mind. We are here with you. Many have made this journey and returned—I have too. You shall do fine. Are you ready?"

Lúlù pulled herself together. "I am ready."

Gbàjà looked intently at Lúlù. "You say that your child speaks to you. Well, you shall find out soon enough. I will ask you one more time: Are you ready to make this journey?"

"I am!" Lúlù answered resolutely. If this inner voice and special power had something to do with her child, she was willing to do whatever was necessary. She lay down in the middle of a circle outlined by shells of different colors.

Everyone but the oracle stood outside the circle.

Gbàjà circled Lúlù and started to chant and wave. "Beni, bring me the water."

The baboon handed Gbàjà a small calabash with dark liquid in it.

Gbàjà sprinkled it on Lúlù. "What time is it?"

Ojúrí rushed outside. "The moon is halfway across the sky."

"Good, now we can begin." Gbàjà started to dance and chant. She drew patterns around Lúlù's eyes with white paint. "You shall see in the spirit with the eyes of your ancestors." She drew patterns on Lúlù's hands. "You shall touch with the hands of your ancestors." She drew patterns on Lúlù's feet. "You shall walk with the feet of your ancestors." Finally, she drew patterns on Lúlù's stomach. "You shall encounter your child in the spirit."

Lúlù gazed at the oracle as her vision grew dim. She closed her eyes.

"Beni, bring the white cloth. Ológun and Ojúrí, come closer." The oracle marked the warriors' hands and feet. "Enter the circle."

Beni handed the cloth to Gbàjà.

"Wrap her from head to toe as you would a corpse," Gbàjà said.

Queen Témbè and Princess Fazilah stared at each other as the warriors wrapped Lúlù from head to toe.

"How shall she breathe?" asked Princess Fazilah.

"Do not worry, Princess. She shall be fine. There is no need for air where she is going. Now, hurry. If this is not done before midnight, the journey may be futile."

Ológun and Ojúrí worked fast to wrap Lúlù.

Lúlù started to scream and shake. Her screams were muffled by the cloth.

"Hold her!" Gbàjà shouted.

Lúlù shouted, "Wele! Wele!"

The shaking turned into a violent quiver, but the warriors held on.

"Weleee!" Her scream faded to a whisper.

The shaking stopped. Princess Fazilah's hand flew to her mouth in horror.

"Leave her alone," Gbàjà said calmly. The oracle examined Lúlù. "It is midnight. She is now dead."

CHAPTER 17

Valley of Shadows

Lúlù opened her eyes. She could see everyone in the room, but they could not see her. She felt a lightness as her body began to lift from the ground. A wave of realization washed over her. Her surroundings slowly became illuminated as she rose higher and started to hear voices.

Lúlù quickly learned to maneuver herself as she floated. She looked down and saw a body wrapped from head to toe in a white cloth. *That must be me.* Gbàjà, the two Mino warriors, the queen, and the princess surrounded her body. She could hear everything they were saying in the land of the living.

The princess anxiously queried, "What happened to her? She was shaking a minute ago, then stopped."

"Princess, she has crossed to the other side," Gbàjà responded.

"You mean she is dead?" Princess Fazilah asked.

"Yes. She shall remain in this state for three days. No one must touch her or unwrap the cloth. Otherwise, we may not be able to bring her back."

"Princess Fazilah, can you hear me?" Lúlù called as she reached out to touch the princess. Her hand went through the princess. Lúlù raised her voice. "Princess! Gbàjà!"

Beni raised his head and looked around.

"Beni, can you hear me?" Lúlù asked.

Beni started to grunt and move around excitedly.

Gbàjà turned to Beni. "What is it?"

The baboon pointed to his ear.

"You hear something?" the oracle inquired.

The baboon nodded. Beni possessed a similar connection to the spirit realm as his master.

By this time, Lúlù had drifted farther away. The figures in the room were getting smaller. Everything became pitch-black. The darkness around her was thick, and the silence was deafening. *This is scary. Where am I?* Thoughts raced through Lúlù's mind. She raised her hands to her face, but she could not see them. She was in a void, surrounded by nothingness. The purpose for her journey slowly drifted back into her mind: she was in the spirit realm to meet the entity behind the voice.

She looked up toward a radiance that was forming above. She accelerated involuntarily toward the light and passed through a portal. She felt a little more in control of herself.

Lúlù drifted through a forest of red leaves, floating a few inches above the ground.

A grotesque creature lumbered down the path in front of her.

This thing is certainly not floating. Is it dead?

Lúlù froze as horror gripped her. She hoped it wouldn't see her if she didn't make a sound. As it approached, Lúlù could see that it was shaped like a man. Its head hung to one side, as if its neck had been snapped, and an oozing stump jutted out from where its right arm should have been.

Lúlù held her breath.

The creature moved parallel to her. Suddenly, it stopped, sniffing the air close to Lúlù.

Lúlù could not control her floating any longer. She slowly descended to the ground. She started to sweat as her feet touched the ground. She closed her eyes in fear.

A moment later, the creature muttered incoherently and shuffled on.

Lúlù opened her eyes. It was definitely the spirit of the dead. Another spirit passed by; this time, it was a woman carrying a crying baby. A few more passed, but they did not seem to notice Lúlù.

These are the spirits of the dead who are suffering, Lúlù thought. *I am in the land of the dead.*

Some of the spirits muttered, and some were quiet. A few of the children cried. Most of the spirits were not audible. She was terrified, but she continued to walk. She tripped over an exposed root and fell. When she looked up, the spirit of a warrior was standing over her. Their eyes locked, which triggered the awareness of all the other spirits.

This cannot be good.

They started stumbling toward her. The one above her reached out to grab her with its bony claws.

Lúlù screamed. A blue beam of light emerged from her mouth and vaporized the spirit.

A second spirit approached.

Lúlù screamed again, and the blue beam came out a second time. Lúlù was now learning to control it. It started in the pit of her stomach and rose to her chest. When her chest glowed with the blue light, she had the ability to open her mouth and project the blue beam. She grew weaker every time she projected. She kept letting the beam out to destroy the attacking spirits until the light started to grow dim. She grew too weak to keep it up.

The remaining spirits, which had taken on a more menacing and evil countenance, closed in on her. Several of them surrounded her and reached down to grab her.

A split second before the spirits touched Lúlù, water burst from the ground. Mónjé's form appeared, lifting her far above the evil spirits. The fountain of water propelled Lúlù into another sphere. The stream of water ceased and took human form. Mónjé appeared before Lúlù.

"Mother?" Lúlù asked.

"It is me, child," Mónjé replied.

Lúlù tried to hug Mónjé, but she walked right through her.

"You cannot touch me, child. I am in the land of the dead now, and you are in the land of the living. You can go back, but I cannot."

"What do you mean, Màmá?"

"I left you at Odùduwà," Mónjé replied. "It's a long story, my child."

"I have nothing but time, Màmá."

Móñjé smiled. "You've grown so much."

Móñjé sat down on a fallen tree with Lúlù and told her all that had transpired after she left.

Lúlù cried through it all.

"It is well, child. It is the will of the gods. We could not have contact otherwise. I shall draw you closer to the other side, but you must keep your distance. I am happy to see you are well. I have watched you from the land of the dead. Things are happening as I knew they would. You are here to discover the voices you are hearing and to understand the powers that are manifesting in you. Some things you shall understand, and some shall be kept hidden from you. Others shall be revealed in mysteries and riddles that you must decipher. I shall lead you some of the way, but some places you must go alone." Móñjé's clothes shone white, and she wore beautiful pearls. Her voice sounded like rushing water.

The two women suddenly appeared on a beach. The waves crashed softly on the shore. As they walked, they came across a long line of people linked by chains, walking toward a boat. Some men were shouting and forcing them to move.

"What does this mean, Màmá?" Lúlù asked.

"This is a sign of things to come, my child. Thousands of people shall be sold into slavery in a foreign land."

They walked away from the waters, and the landscape changed. They were now in a village where people gathered around a golden stool.

A man dressed in a brightly colored wrapper and beads stood beside the stool. Everyone around him bowed.

"Who is that, Màmá?" Lúlù asked.

"Those are the Ashanti people. The golden stool represents the power they possess. They shall be allies in the struggles to come."

Móñjé and Lúlù walked until they came upon a rocky hill. They climbed to the top and looked down the other side to see a battle. Fires burned in several places. Screams were heard everywhere.

"Who are those people fighting?" Lúlù asked.

"Those are our people," Móñjé replied.

"Which ones?" Lúlù asked.

"This is where I must leave you, child. I have said and done all I can. I shall continue to watch over you. You shall live a good life." Móńjé started to fade away. "Go down the valley and continue your journey. I love you, little fawn." Móńjé waved at Lúlù.

"Please, don't leave me, Màmá!" Lúlù shouted.

Móńjé evaporated like steam and vanished before Lúlù could even take a step. Lúlù was alone again. She felt despondent. She looked down at the battlefield, took a deep breath, and proceeded down the mountain.

The dead warriors resembled the warriors from Odùduwà. She also saw dead warriors from Dahomey. She remembered Móńjé's words: *These are our people.* Lúlù paused and looked around. Several battles were being waged at the same time. People of other races fought bitterly, using weapons she had never seen before that made loud, scary noises.

A tall man stood up and shouted, "Cease!"

The fighting continued.

"Cease!"

Some people took notice, but the fighting did not stop.

"Cease!"

A black lion appeared beside him. It roared so loudly that everything on the battlefield shook.

The battles came to a halt.

The man bellowed his message: "We have done enough fighting and have gained little from it. Now, we shall stop this madness. I have a claim to the throne by the virtue of my birth. You shall live in peace with your neighbors. If anyone wishes to challenge this, speak now." He surveyed the warriors on the battlefield. "If you shall not have me as your king, challenge me now." The man was big and tall. His black skin was marked with sweat and blood.

The smoke in the air blurred Lúlù's view of the man.

The lion roared again, and the battlefield shook.

No one challenged the man.

"Then forever hold your peace." He raised his spear with both hands above his head and drove it into the ground.

A crack in the ground appeared. Everyone followed the path of the crack.

Lúlù heard drums and people singing in the distance. Her gaze followed the crack until it stopped between her feet.

Everyone looked at her.

Lúlù's gaze met the leader's gaze.

"Mother!" He stretched out his hand.

The drums became deafening. People and elements converged simultaneously.

A woman on a dark horse appeared, carrying a spear. She was headed straight for Lúlù. Lúlù's body started to glow with a soft white light.

A second before impact, the black lion lunged and attacked the woman. Blood splattered onto Lúlù's clothes. Everything went dark.

CHAPTER 18

Knowledge and Realms

Back at Gbàjà's hut, Queen Témbè turned to Gbàjà. "We shall return the day after tomorrow."

"Very well, my queen," Gbàjà replied.

Queen Témbè and Princess Fazilah left Gbàjà's hut and headed back to the palace. Two palace guards trailed behind them.

"Now, my daughter, I am eager to hear of your studies in Timbuktu."

"Mother, I learned so much listening to the scholars and teachers. People come from all over the world to learn from the scholars. I saw men with skin like bronze. I also saw men with skin like milk. We learned that there is one God. All embrace Islam and stand for peace and justice. You would be amazed at what is happening in the city too. The buildings are like nothing I have seen before. And the social and technological advancement!"

Queen Témbè looked at her daughter with pride. "I shall take you to visit Abyssinia. There is yet much to learn. We have Christianity over there too. People there believe in one God. That was even before Islam. There are churches built into rocks. I am of the lineage of King Solomon, the son of King David. You are connected to that lineage too, Fazilah. Christianity and Islam speak of him."

The princess grew even more excited. "That is Suleiman in the Quran!"

"There are things I shall tell you because you are now of age," said the queen. "There was a great queen in Abyssinia. Her name was Sheba. She was an exceptionally beautiful and intelligent woman. She went to Jerusalem to see King Solomon, considered the wisest man in the world. He was blessed by the one true God, and many kings of the world paid homage to him. The queen traveled many days in a long caravan." Queen Témbè shared the story of the queen of Sheba, how she had spent time with King Solomon, and how they were intrigued by each other. "Their relationship produced a son, Menelik, and the queen of Sheba brought him home with her."

Princess Fazilah listened with rapt attention.

Queen Témbè continued, "When they left Jerusalem, they took the Ark of the Covenant and brought it to Abyssinia."

"What is the Ark of the Covenant?" Princess Fazilah asked.

The queen described the ark and the power it held. "No one has seen the ark since. It is held and protected by high priests in Abyssinia."

"Is it still in Abyssinia?" the princess asked.

"Yes, but if the wrong person sees or touches it, they will die instantly," the queen said. "The priests are renowned and propagate the teaching of one God as taught by King Solomon. He was a man of true wisdom. I know of the Christian and Islamic teachings—and the knowledge and advancement of Timbuktu. The king of the Songhai Empire is a man of exceeding wealth. The world has many mysteries, my daughter, and it is hard to comprehend them all." Queen Témbè stopped and looked at Princess Fazilah.

"Mother, I never knew you know so much. You never talked about this great heritage. Why?"

"When you take on a husband, you take on his culture. As queen, I am an ambassador of his heritage."

"Then what do you say about these practices and rituals we have now?"

"I shall say this. The land of Alkebulan (Africa) is vast. Many kingdoms exist in it, including our own and the kingdom of my father. You must travel to understand. From what I hear, there are great cities in the south with great walls. There are mighty warriors and powerful weapons. To the east and to the north, there are edifices called pyramids, which are of monumental height. No other kingdom knows the technology they used. There are significant medicinal advancements and wise philosophers. Religions have existed for thousands of years that teach us of one God. The stories are similar in many ways. It is important to learn about them and have a broad understanding of life. The practices here in Dahomey have their powers too ... as you have seen."

"Then what is the way?" Princess Fazilah asked.

Queen Témbè looked directly at the princess. "Wherever success and advancement are found, that is where the way lies. By their fruits, you shall know them."

Two Mino warriors guarded Gbàjà's hut. Ojúrí sat inside near Lúlù's wrapped body. It was morning.

Ológun led Gbàjà on one of the many forest paths. Birds with vibrant blue, green, and red feathers chirped in the trees. The morning breeze was cool.

"So, what happens now?" asked Ológun.

Gbàjà replied, "As I said earlier, we wait. Lúlù is on a journey. She shall see and encounter many things. She must not be disturbed. Ensure that your guards remain at the entrance of my hut. No one can enter until the three-day period has expired."

Ológun said, "I saw this ceremony as a little girl, but I do not remember who it was performed for."

"It was for me," Gbàjà replied.

Ológun raised her eyebrows and gazed at Gbàjà in admiration.

Gbàjà said, "To be an oracle, you must die and return—after which you shall have great abilities and shall be taught the ways of our ancestors. It is not as common a practice as it was in the days of old. Some people went and never returned. Some went mad, especially if they were disturbed in their death. It is not easy to be on the other side."

"Then why put this woman through such an ordeal?"Ológun asked.

They came to a fork in the path, andOlógun motioned for Gbàjà to take the left trail.

"Do you remember the signs in the forest that led us to her?" Gbàjà asked.

"I remember," Ológun replied.

"Bats flying under a full moon are noteworthy. She is significant—more so than you may realize. The gods have given me inclinations about her. I am helping us gain clarity about what is to come."

"What did you see when you were on the other side?" Ológun asked.

"I do not like to dwell on those memories," Gbàjà replied solemnly.

"We are all intrigued. And as a warrior, I may cross over someday. I wonder what I shall find on the other side." Ológun walked beside the oracle with her hands behind her back.

Little animals scurried in the undergrowth as the humans approached.

"There are many dimensions on the other side, Ológun. Where we go during the ritual is the valley of the shadow of death. It is a temporary death; under the right circumstances, one can return. In that realm, the living and the dead interact. You see elements of both worlds. The spirits that inhabit that realm can communicate with you. Some of them are in transition to permanent death—a place of no return. Some have gotten stuck on their journey because of unfinished matters they have here on earth. Images are sometimes blurry and vague."

"That does not sound like an enjoyable place. What about the paradise that we hear of?"

"Paradise, or purgatory, is a permanent realm. That is not where Lúlù is at this time. She is in the realm where the world of man and spirit intersect. One must understand the principles to navigate the realms."

Ológun let out a long breath. "I learn more every day. This life is complex."

"That it is, great warrior, that it is," the oracle affirmed.

Suddenly, Beni became agitated. He jumped up and down, pointing back in the direction of Gbàjà's hut.

Gbàjà studied Beni. "Something is not right."

92

"What do you mean?" Ológun asked.

Gbàjà ignored her question. "Beni, what do you perceive?"

The baboon kept pointing frantically in the direction of Gbàjà's hut.

After a few moments, Gbàjà discerned Beni's sign. She knew her baboon well. "Ah! Lúlù's body! She is in grave danger. We must head back at once!"

Ológun was already skipping through falling trees and shrubs, picking up speed through the forest.

Gbàjà hurriedly climbed onto Beni's back and followed Ológun.

Jantaa and Dìran reached Gbàjà's hut and crouched in the bushes nearby.

"They've all left. Now is the time to strike," Dìran whispered.

"You are right. She cannot survive if we strike her now. But what about the warriors by the door?" Jantaa asked.

"We shall find an entrance through the back," Dìran responded.

Jantaa and Dìran crept into Gbàjà's hut through a small opening at the back. They saw Lúlù on the floor with a Mino warrior seated on a wooden stool beside her. The Mino warrior's back was positioned in their direction, giving them an advantage to strike a death blow without much obstruction. Dìran quietly signaled to Jantaa to pull out his cutlass. He made a motion to cut off the Mino warrior's head.

Jantaa nodded and quietly pulled out his cutlass. He stepped closer to the Mino warrior and swung rapidly.

Ojúrí had pretended not to notice their entry. She swiftly pushed backwards and leaned sideways as she slipped under Jantaa's arm, avoiding his weapon. She thrust her own dagger into his lower chest before she hit the floor.

Jantaa tried to shelter the impact, but he yelled out in pain as he crashed to the floor.

Ojúrí quickly rolled backward toward Dìran, who had already stepped forward to stab her with his spear. Ojúrí spun sideways, blocked Dìran's spear with the wrought iron shield around her wrist, and swung an ax into his side before he could move out of the way.

Dìran muttered in agony.

In the heat of the commotion, Jantaa crawled to Lúlù's side, pulled out a dagger, and raised his hand to deal Lúlù a fatal blow. Two arrows flew rapidly from the Mino warriors by the door. One passed through his chest, and the other pierced his left eye. Jantaa dropped his dagger and gasped in pain. His end had come.

Mónjé's judgment had come upon them sooner than he expected. Mónjé's water image flashed through his mind—as he slumped to the floor and breathed his last.

Dìran was weak from the ax wound in his side, but he was resilient and determined to finish the mission. He pulled out his dagger, rallied, and sprang toward Ojúrí.

Just at that moment, Ológun burst into the hut and thrust her spear at Dìran's head. Her spear pierced Dìran's forehead and pushed his brain out the back of his head. His body dropped to the ground with a heavy thud.

Beni entered with Gbàjà.

"Did anything or anyone touch her body?" Gbàjà asked worriedly.

"Never. There is not one scratch on her, Mà," Ojúrí assured.

Ológun was still breathing heavily.

"Who are these men?" Ológun demanded. She retrieved her spear from Dìran's head.

"We do not know, but I expect they are from the kingdom of Odùduwà," Ojúrí answered.

"Whoever they are, I am sure they are after Lúlù's life," Gbàjà stated grimly.

Queen Témbè and Princess Fazilah returned to Gbàjà's hut at sundown on the third day.

Gbàjà, Ológun, and Ojúrí were already present. They showed the queen and princess the bodies of the two dead spies and recounted the event. The royal pair was notably alarmed by the occurrence and concerned for Lúlù's safety.

Princess Fazilah peppered the warriors with questions. "She is not back yet. Is she okay? Was her body hurt?"

"Her body is well. She shall return in due time, Princess. In due time," Gbàjà replied calmly.

Suddenly, Lúlù's wrapped body began to glow.

The queen and the princess exchanged an astonished look.

Lúlù began to move. She struggled to extricate herself from the wrapped cloths.

"Help her!" Gbàjà exclaimed.

Ológun and Ojúrí rushed to Lúlù's wrapped body and began to cut her loose from the linen.

Princess Fazilah froze in fear and amazement. She had never seen anything like this before.

Lúlù struggled out of the wraps and gagged. She removed the cloth from her mouth and nostrils and gasped for air. The glow from her body dimmed. She whispered, "Water, water … please!" She struggled to catch her breath.

Gbàjà motioned to Beni. "Hurry, get her some water."

Beni brought Lúlù water in a calabash.

She grabbed it and started to drink hastily. The water ran down the sides of her mouth, along her neck, and disappeared between her breasts.

"Can someone please explain what I'm witnessing?" Princess Fazilah asked.

"Not now, Princess," Gbàjà replied curtly.

Ológun and Ojúrí helped Lúlù up.

Gbàjà said, "Lúlù must readjust to the realm of the living. She shall need our help. She may choose to share all, part, or none of what she saw. The choice is hers."

Beni grunted and stared at Lúlù.

Lúlù took a few steps and fell.

Beni lunged forward and grabbed her before she hit the ground. He cradled Lúlù in his arms as he walked slowly toward the guest chambers.

Ológun looked at Gbàjà and shrugged. The party followed Beni.

Later that evening, Gbàjà, Ológun, Ojúrí, Princess Fazilah, King Drogba, Queen Témbè, and Elder Bira gathered at the palace with the two dead bodies. To avoid panic among the people, no one else was invited.

Ojúrí informed King Drogba of all that had occurred at Gbàjà's hut.

King Drogba ordered that the dead bodies be thrown into a pit in the forest. He appointed two skilled Mino warriors to protect Lúlù wherever she went.

Even though Dìran and Jantaa were warriors, they were buried dishonorably because of Mónjé's judgment and curse upon them.

A few days later, Múrí learned the fate of the two Odùduwà warriors from a palace guard. He sent another raven to deliver the bad news to Kúyè.

Kúyè was unsettled for many full moons. *This task is much harder than I anticipated. Perhaps I should let the matter rest for now.* Nonetheless, the news haunted him like a nightmare.

CHAPTER 19

Princes Are Born

For many full moons, Lúlù remained quiet about her encounter. No one pressured her. As Gbàjà had advised, she should not be forced to disclose. It could bring a curse to whomever forced the message. Her daily routines changed. She kept more to herself as she tried to make sense of it all.

By the sixth full moon of the year, Lúlù was in the full term of her pregnancy.

Queen Témbé, Gbàjà, Princess Fazilah, and Lúlù were weaving mats in the queen's chamber. It was one of the queen's pastimes, and the palace was strewn with her beautiful designs and creations. Lúlù's words cut through the lighthearted chatter.

"I saw my son as a grown man," Lúlù said in a high-pitched voice.

The women went silent.

She narrated some of what she had encountered in the spirit realm. As she was concluding the narrative, her belly began to glow a faint blue. Lúlù held her belly and gasped. She had an agonizing look on her face.

"I believe my child is coming," Lúlù whispered through the pain.

Gbàjà and Princess Fazilah helped Lúlù into one of the palace rooms.

Lúlù's labor progressed over the next eight hours.

The queen's maids and midwives stood by, encouraging her to push and rest as the contractions ebbed and flowed like the tide.

Queen Témbè held Lúlù's hand. "It's almost over, Lúlù. Give it a big push."

Lúlù was exhausted from pushing and dripping in sweat. She took a deep breath and pushed one last time.

The little prince came out screaming.

Lúlù gazed at her newborn lovingly. "You shall be called Adébòwálé because you shall return to rule your people."

Queen Témbè and Princess Fazilah smiled.

The queen looked at Lúlù and nodded slowly. "He shall be called Adébòwálé."

Queen Adélolá sat in her chamber with her maidservants. Her stomach had ballooned so much that she could no longer see her feet when she stood. Queen Adélolá was expected to deliver any day.

King Àjosè entered the queen's chamber. The queen nodded to her maidservants to excuse them.

"How are you feeling today, my queen?"

"I am well, my king. I'm eager for this little prince to come out." She rubbed her stomach.

The king smiled and caressed the queen's stomach. "Me too, my dear. How do you know it's a prince?"

"Because he kicks like you," the queen replied wryly.

"If he kicks like me, he is destined for greatness." The king beamed.

"Have you thought of a name yet?" the queen asked.

The king cleared his throat. "I have."

The queen scowled at him.

"You have not given it a thought, have you?" the queen asked.

The king's smile returned. "How about Àjosè II?"

The baby kicked, and the queen leaned forward in pain.

"Lolá?" King Àjosè looked alarmed.

The queen tried to stand. The lower part of her garment was soaked with bodily fluids.

"I believe it is time. We shall soon meet our son."

The full moon shone brightly into the room.

As was customary, the queen's labor was announced. Word spread quickly throughout the kingdom that the royal delivery had started. The citizens of Odùduwà were expected to pray for the queen and the child's safe delivery.

Four midwives arrived to assist in the delivery. They asked the king to leave the room. King Àjosè stood outside the queen's chambers, pacing back and forth with his hands gripped behind his back. His body trembled with a mix of excitement and apprehension. The hours that ensued felt like an eternity.

Kúyè also paced back and forth outside the queen's chamber.

At long last, one of the midwives stepped out of the room, sweating and covered in blood.

The cry of the newborn rang out behind the midwife.

King Àjosè's heart leaped at the sound of the child's cry, but he sensed something was wrong. He turned to the midwife. "Is everything all right? What did she have?"

"The queen has given birth to a boy, my king." The midwife hesitated before continuing. "The baby is fine, but there is a problem."

A lump formed in King Àjosè's throat.

"My king, the queen has lost much blood. I must find more warm water and clean cloths. You cannot enter yet." The midwife hurried off.

The king ignored the midwife and pushed into the room.

Kúyè waited outside the queen's chamber.

The queen was lying on the bed in the bloodstained sheets.

The second midwife was kneeling beside her, holding the newborn prince. She bowed to the king and handed him the newborn.

"What happened?" King Àjosè asked.

"The strain of the pushing caused a rupture. She lost a large amount of blood, my king. We stopped the bleeding, but she is not well, my king. Let us pray to the gods that she survives."

The king held the newborn with joy, but he felt gripped with fear. "What can be done to make her well?" He gave the newborn prince back to one of the midwives. "Elder Kúyè!"

Kúyè rushed in. "Your Highness?"

"Please send for Bàbá Fádèyí at once!"

"Yes, Your Highness." Kúyè stepped out and called one of the guards. "Òdígí!"

"Yes, my lord?" Òdígí answered.

"Call for Bàbá Fádèyí at once."

"Very well, my lord." The guard hurried off on one of the royal horses.

Fádèyí was the king's seer, the traditional head priest to the gods, and an oracle in Odùduwà. He was a man of old age with great wisdom and knowledge of the things of the spirit.

Fádèyí rushed to the king's palace. He arrived in his white dashiki, *fìlà*, and shóóró. Fádèyí commanded respect wherever he went, and his knowledge made him invaluable to the king.

Guards, maidservants, and fellow elders greeted Fádèyí as he entered the palace gate.

With his wealth of experience, Fádèyí had helped the kingdom avert disaster several times. He was one of the few who could challenge the king and pronounce a course of action that the king would seriously consider. Fádèyí dismounted his white horse.

The king greeted him and called him into the queen's chamber.

"I feel a spirit hovering here," Fádèyí said as he entered.

King Àjosè glanced around the room, confused.

Fádèyí stood beside the queen's bed. He took out his ifá oracle (cowrie shells), threw them on a piece of brown cloth on the floor, and began to chant. He touched the queen's hands with his oracle staff and looked at the queen intently. He threw the cowrie shells inside a calabash, nodded, and grunted. "Your Highness?"

"What is it, Bàbá Fádèyí?"

"A spirit is trying to drag the queen to the other side. It is an oracle's spirit—and the queen owes it a debt."

"What debt? I shall pay whatever is required," the king said.

"It is a spiritual debt. Your wealth is of no value in the spirit realm. I shall bring her back, but this will not be the last time this spirit shall make demands."

"Which of the oracles, Bàbá Fádèyí?"

"I am not permitted to disclose the oracle, Your Highness. The gods shall reveal it when the time comes."

The king was not satisfied with the response, but he was not going to question the gods.

Fádèyí started chanting again, applying a black powder to the queen's feet and forehead. *"Eni tó wo lé tí ò ká gò lo yi ń ta. Mo kí o ní lé, mo kí à le jò kí n tó wo lé o"* (A person who enters a domain without acknowledging the owner stands the risk of getting stung. I acknowledge the owner and guest before I proceed). "Grant me the power to bring her back."

After several minutes of incantations, Fádèyí rose and gathered his things. "She shall pull through, Your Highness. Yet, sooner or later, the gods shall request a sacrifice to prevent a royal calamity."

King Àjosè shook his head, bewildered. "I do not understand."

"We shall discuss this at a later time," Fádèyí said.

King Àjosè pressed, "Bàbá Fádèyí, please help me understand."

Fádèyí hesitated and then said, "Something bad may befall Odùduwà if a sacrifice is not provided soon, Your Highness."

"But what type of sacrifice, Bàbá Fádèyí?"

Fádèyí looked at the king. "The gods shall give us direction when the time comes, Your Highness." He packed up his ifá oracle, picked up his staff, and headed out the door.

As a sign of respect, King Àjosè accompanied Fádèyí to the palace entrance, and then he hurried back to the queen's chamber.

To his surprise, the queen had already sat up. Fádèyí's intervention had brought her back. Àjosè looked quizzically at the midwives.

The midwives shook their heads. "Her Highness was sitting up before we entered, Your Highness."

"What happened?" the queen asked weakly.

King Àjosè said, "You lost a lot of blood. You did not respond for a while. Thank the gods you are back."

"Where is my son?" the queen asked.

"Your son is well. The maids are taking good care of him," King Àjosè replied.

"May I see him?" the queen urged.

The king called in the direction of the guards. "Òdígí! Get the queen's maids to bring the prince at once."

"Yes, my king." Òdígí hurried off.

The maids brought the little prince to Queen Adélolá. She nestled her son in her arms and gazed at him in wonder. "You shall be called Adébáyò because you completed my joy."

The king nodded in agreement. "He shall be called Adébáyò."

Nine full moons had passed since Mónjé's murder. Life had hummed along slowly and naturally in Odùduwà. The gods had remained quiet.

All looked well on the surface, but the oracles of the land could hear the cries of the innocent blood that had been spilled. The peace that Odùduwà had enjoyed for years would soon be shattered.

CHAPTER 20

Fear and Guilt

In the Odùduwà kingdom, royalty and citizens alike prepared for the prince's naming ceremony. According to custom, the prince was to be officially named on the eighth day after his birth. The citizens of Odùduwà kingdom were filled with excitement and joy. After a dull and gloomy dry season, the people had a reason to celebrate.

Cattle were brought into the slaughterhouse. Numerous varieties of yams, plantains, and wines were packed in the storehouses in preparation for the ceremony.

Contrary to the norm, Queen Adélolá did not participate in the planning. She hung around her chamber as special maids cared for the little prince. Lúlù consumed her mind. The queen dearly missed her company.

Two days before the naming ceremony, the queen stood on her terrace, staring at the pristinely maintained gardens below. She could not stop thinking about Lúlù. She felt like she had let Lúlù down by going along with Kúyè's plan. She felt overwhelmed with guilt. She should not have let her leave the palace. *But I was not aware of her leaving,* she reasoned. *Elder Kúyè orchestrated it all. Even still, I could have brought Lúlù back instead of leaving it in Kúyè's hands.*

A maid interrupted her thoughts. "Your Highness, it is time for the little prince to feed."

After the little prince was breastfed, the queen returned him to one of the maids and turned to another. "Please call for Elder Kúyè at once."

"Yes, my queen." The maid left the queen's chamber, passing two other maids in the foyer.

The two maids stopped as the queen's maid strode away.

"The queen has been acting strange lately," the first maid said.

The second maid nodded. "I passed her in the courts a few days ago, and she was staring off into the distance. She seemed worried about something."

"I thought she would be excited since she has waited so long to have an heir. And she used to make everyone around her so happy."

"Did you hear the rumors?"

"What rumors?"

The second maid leaned closer. "About Lúlù. Do you know—"

"Get moving!" The head maid walked by, her large frame rolling from side to side as she moved. "You have no work to do? Go help take the food to the storehouse. Then you shall scrub the court floors until I can see myself in them!"

"Yes, Mà." They hurried along before her thick hands could reach them.

Big Màmá's slaps were legendary and painful. She was a no-nonsense woman and commanded respect from all the maids. She had been in the palace for as long as the maids could remember. She hailed from the same village as Lúlù.

Moments later, the queen's maid entered Queen Adélolá's chamber with Elder Kúyè.

"Leave us, and take the prince with you," the queen instructed.

"Yes, Your Highness."

The queen turned to Kúyè. "I believe Lúlù would have delivered her child by now. Gather some men at once and go to Sàbẹ. Bring her and her child back to the palace."

"I have already done so, my queen," Kúyè replied.

"Thank you, my lord."

Kúyè took a deep breath and cleared his throat. "Yes, my queen. Two full moons ago, I sent men to Sàbẹ to check on her and invite her back, but ... my queen. She ..."

"She what, Elder Kúyè?"

"The men returned with bad news, my queen. They were told she ran away. Her mother has not been seen for a while, and their hut and the surrounding lands are flooded with a powerful river."

The queen fainted.

Kúyè stretched out his hands and caught the queen before she hit the floor. "Your Highness!" He turned to the entrance and yelled, "Maids! Maids!"

Some maids in the foyer rushed into the queen's chamber and carried her to her bed.

"Call for the physician at once!" Kúyè bellowed.

"Yes, my lord." One of the maids hurried off.

Within moments, the native physician arrived and examined the queen. "She shall be fine. She is simply fatigued. She must rest well. And she must not be distressed."

"Thank you." Kúyè turned to the maids. "Make sure that no one disturbs her." He walked out of the queen's chamber with a discreet smirk. He had finally put the queen's mind to rest about Lúlù.

CHAPTER 21

A Ray of Hope

One day before the ceremony, gifts and congratulatory messages arrived from ally kingdoms and villages that surrounded Odùduwà. The Ashanti kingdom, which had been an ally for decades, sent gold and expensive jewelry. Even Guguwa, the king of the Hawani kingdom who had disrespected King Àjosè, sent gifts and a warm congratulatory message to the king and queen.

Each kingdom demonstrated its joy over the birth of the little prince. But no messages or gifts arrived from the Dahomey kingdom. King Àjosè did not show much concern for Dahomey's disregard, but he took note of it.

On the eighth day, the sun rose gloriously, shedding light on Odùduwà's environs and waking flora and fauna with its warm touch. The excitement in the air was palpable. The kingdom's citizenry bustled with expectation. Important guests and dignitaries arrived on horses and carriages from far and wide.

The guests glittered in their adornment as they made their way through the palace corridors to the banquet hall.

The king of Ashanti took his seat at the high table with his queen.

King Guguwa of Hawani sat with his queen.

The seats reserved for the king and queen of Dahomey were conspicuously empty.

The king found the head of the guards. "Have the guests arrived from Dahomey?"

"No, my king," the guard replied.

I shall address this later, the king thought. *Dahomey is getting bolder. But tonight, we celebrate.*

Masqueraders began to entertain the crowd. The drummers of Odùduwà were legendary. The drums chanted rhythmically. People had little choice but to sway and shake to the undulating rhythm.

King Àjosè stood up as one of the guards blew a horn.

The music came to a halt.

King Àjosè raised his jar of palm wine. "Your Majesties. My honored guests. The kingdom of Odùduwà thanks you for being here. I want to thank everyone who has come from far and near to honor this occasion. My queen and I thank you! May we all continue to increase in strength and number by the blessings of the gods of our land."

"Àsheeee!" the people answered.

"As you are aware, I have long awaited an heir, and I have been questioned by some." Àjosè paused for a second and scanned the crowd.

A few guests grunted their agreement.

"The gods have deemed it fit to bless the Odùduwà kingdom with this bundle of joy that brings us hope. We shall enjoy continued peace and prosperity."

The king paused and glanced at the queen. She seemed uninterested, but she forced a smiled as she caught the king's gaze. Her mind kept wandering to Lúlù and her child, but she had to focus on the ceremony.

"As is tradition in our culture, we shall name the prince today—the eighth day of his birth." The king beckoned to Bàbá Fádèyí to dedicate the child to the gods and pronounce his names.

Fádèyí stood in front of the king and queen, holding the child in the air as he made affirmative declarations. When finished, he called out the names of the prince for the crowd to hear and acknowledge.

After the naming, each dignitary came forward to congratulate King Àjosè and Queen Adélolá.

King Guguwa of the Hawani kingdom approached King Àjosè. The queen scrutinized him as he approached.

Kúyè stood to the right of the queen's throne, regarding Guguwa with equal intensity.

When Guguwa was a few steps from King Àjosè, two of the king's guards blocked his path with their spears.

King Àjosè gestured for them to stand down.

King Guguwa addressed King Àjosè. "My lord, I want to personally congratulate you for giving us a ray of hope. I want to take this opportunity to apologize for the seemingly abrasive way in which I addressed you about an heir. It was for good intention, but I suspect it was misinterpreted." He gave Àjosè a slight hug. He had a suspicious expression about him. He turned to the queen. "Your Highness, congratulations on the little prince's arrival. May he continue to be a source of joy to us all."

"Àsheee. Thank you, my lord, and thank you for coming," the queen replied.

King Guguwa nodded, smiled, and walked down the steps.

King Àjosè gasped. His eyes rolled into his skull, and he collapsed, convulsing violently.

Queen Adélolá jumped up and knelt beside her unconscious husband. She glowered at King Guguwa in rage. "Seize him at once!" she bellowed.

Dòngárì and Òdígí grabbed King Guguwa. Three other guards rushed to help King Àjosè.

"How could he?" an Odùduwà chief exclaimed in disbelief.

"I always knew he was evil," another Odùduwà chief replied.

"He should be killed!" the first chief affirmed vehemently.

"This may instigate a war. Hawani is a big kingdom," the second chief speculated.

The queen of Hawani screamed in protest as guards carried her husband away.

Dòngárì and Òdígí dragged Guguwa to the dungeon, and Kúyè followed close behind.

King Guguwa was beside himself. "You have made a mistake!" he thundered. "Odùduwà shall pay dearly for it! You shall feel the wrath of Hawani!"

"Shut your mouth!" Kúyè shouted.

The guards shoved King Guguwa into the dungeon and slammed the door.

CHAPTER 22

An Enemy Within

King Àjosè clung to life in his chambers.

Queen Adélolá, Kúyè, and the king's closest advisers, seers, and palace physicians stood by his side.

"Bàbá Fádèyí, is he going to live?" the queen asked.

"Let us ask the ifá oracle." Fádèyí took out his ifá oracle and sat down on the floor.

Kúyè and the king's advisers watched motionless.

Fádèyí touched the king's hands and legs with his ifá cowrie shells and spread them on a cloth. He pronounced some incantations and shook his head.

"What is it?" Queen Adélolá asked.

"There is an enemy within, my queen," Fádèyí replied. "The king's sudden ailment was provoked by the gods due to an enemy within the kingdom." He paused. "Hmm. The ifá says the ant that is destroying the plant lives on the plant. I do not believe King Guguwa is involved in this issue. Perhaps now is the time to make a sacrifice to the gods."

Kúyè trembled as fear coursed through his veins. He suddenly felt very weak, but he concealed his discomfort.

Queen Adélolá felt disappointed that King Guguwa had nothing to do with the matter. She wanted to punish him for disrespecting her husband during the Odùduwà festival. Now that the opportunity had presented itself, she was not ready to let him go.

"My queen, it is possible for him to recover," Fádèyí said.

"Please continue, Bàbá," Queen Adélolá said.

"We must prepare a sacrifice and carry it to *Odò Ọba* (Ọba River) before seven days pass. If the sacrifice floats away in the river, the king shall be healed. If it remains at the riverbank, we may lose him."

The Odò Ọba was the largest river in the Odùduwà kingdom.

"What do we need for the sacrifice, Bàbá Fádèyí?" the queen asked.

Fádèyí placed his cowrie shells on the floor to consult the gods again. "We must gather seven fresh leaves from a poisonous plant in the Àìmò Forest, three eggs of a giant lizard that resides in the cave of Olúwéré, and the skin of a python that resides in the forest of Irúnmolè. This snake crawls out of its skin every fortnight on the new masquerade festival to take human form, but it returns to the forest and to its skin when morning breaks."

Adélolá felt overwhelmed with all that Fádèyí had stated. She took a deep breath and called out to one of the king's trusted guards. "Dòngárì!"

Dòngárì was the palace head guard, and he was also in charge of the kingdom's foreign affairs.

The head guard rushed to the queen's side and knelt on one knee. "Yes, my queen?"

"Get me the general at once!"

Dòngárì ran to the royal stables and rode off with his spear. He traversed winding paths until he reached Àjàmú's hut near the border of Odùduwà. "The queen summons you, my lord."

Àjàmú emerged from his hut, surprised at the guard's arrival. "Dòngárì?"

"Yes, my lord," Dòngárì answered. "The queen requests your presence at once, my lord."

"Certainly. I hope all is well at the palace." Àjàmú had always been a man of courage and character. He tucked his dagger and ax into his loincloth, climbed on his horse, and followed Dòṅgárì back to the palace.

Queen Adélolá paced back and forth until Dòṅgárì and Àjàmú returned. The queen met them at the edge of the courts. "Àjàmú, welcome. Thank you for coming on such short notice."

He bowed. "It is always an honor to serve, Your Highness."

Queen Adélolá extended her arms. "Please rise, Àjàmú. I can always rely on you. Please, come with me." She led Àjàmú into King Àjosè's room.

Àjàmú's eyes widened in shock. "What has happened to His Highness?"

"This is why I have called you here, General." Queen Adélolá quickly recounted the evening's events. She looked at Fádèyí and nodded respectfully. "Bàbá Fádèyí, you may explain the sacrifice."

"Certainly, Your Highness. The gods are not happy with our land. Therefore, this tragedy has befallen us. We must prepare a sacrifice to appease the gods and the oracle spirits." Fádèyí detailed the three sacrifices again.

Queen Adélolá looked hopefully at Àjàmú. "Is it possible to gather these sacrifices?"

Àjàmú took a deep breath. "It can be done, Your Highness. It must be done. I have thousands of warriors under my command. How many warriors do you need for the mission?"

Fádèyí spread his ifá oracle on the floor again. "Hmmm. *Odù méta* (Three baskets of sacred wisdom). "Ifá only requested three warriors for this mission, and the mission must be carried out in secret."

"Very well. I shall send for two of my bravest warriors. And I shall personally oversee the mission, Your Highness," he replied.

"Thank you, General. You have remained a faithful friend and loyal to the throne. But I do not want you to leave your role as general vacant."

Àjàmú thought for a moment. "Very well, Your Highness. I shall appoint three trusted warriors of Odùduwà for the mission. I believe they shall be successful."

Àjàmú addressed Fádèyí. "How long do we have?"

"We have six days to obtain the sacrifices. The seventh day, we must carry it to Odò Ọba before it is too late."

Àjàmú turned to Dòngárì. "Call for Àjàní, Labí, and Dépò at once."

"My lord." Dòngárì nodded and rode off.

Àjàmú turned to Fádèyí. "You say there is a curse. If I may ask, who or what has brought this curse on Odùduwà? As far as I know, we have observed all the festivals and rites. Whoever has brought the curse must be identified."

Kúyè's heart raced.

"We shall address that at a later time, General. For now, we must expend every effort to preserve the life of His Highness."

At dawn the following day, Dòngárì returned to the palace with Àjàní, Labí, and Dépò.

Queen Adélolá, Àjàmú, and Fádèyí met the warriors in the king's court.

"You are welcome, warriors of Odùduwà," the queen greeted.

They bowed. "It is an honor to serve, Your Highness."

"Please stand. You must have had a long ride to the palace. Please sit."

"Thank you, Your Highness." The three warriors sat down.

Àjàmú addressed the warriors. "Àjàníogun!"

Àjàní responded, "General."

"Jagunlabì!"

Labí echoed, "General."

"Ògúndépò!"

Dépò repeated, "General."

"Thank you, warriors of Odùduwà, for your unfailing loyalty and service to the throne and the kingdom." He relayed the mission.

When Àjàmú finished, the warriors stood. "We are ready to carry out the task, my lord."

Àjàmú smiled with pride and nodded in approval. He turned to Queen Adélolá and Fádèyí. "They are ready, Your Highness."

"Very well." Fádèyí stood up. "Ifá has informed me that a seven-day masquerade festival will soon commence in the neighboring villages.

This shall work in your favor for a portion of your mission—to retrieve the skin of the python." Fádèyí shared further details and words of advice for their perilous mission.

The warriors nodded and committed the instructions to memory.

Fádèyí gave the three warriors black powders and potions in small bottles for any obstacle they might encounter. He prepared them for the journey and blessed the warriors. "The gods of Odùduwà shall protect and guide you."

The warriors cried, "Àsheee!"

As they bowed, the queen pronounced her blessing on them and touched each of their heads with the king's scepter. "You shall go and come back well. May the gods be with you, my warriors."

Àjàmú gave Àjàní a look of approval.

Àjàní looked at Labí and Dépò and shouted, "Warriors!"

They raised their weapons. "Eeeeeee!"

"Warriors!"

"Eeeeeee!"

"Warriors of Odùduwà!"

"Eeeeeee!"

Àjàní addressed his comrades. "It is time to show our strength once again. Now, let us go and take these items with authority." He headed out.

Labí and Dépò followed, shouting and singing, "*Jagunjagun ló ń bò! Jagunjagun ló ń bò! Olórì ogun kìí ń bèrù ogun! Jagunjagun ló ń bò!*" (The warriors are coming! The warriors are coming! A brave warrior does not run from battle! The warriors are coming!)

Àjàmú looked on with pride as the three young warriors rode off into the forest.

The urgency of the sacrifice propelled the warriors forward. They rode as fast as they could in the direction of the Àìmò Forest. The only way to enter the Àìmò Forest was through the Abàmì River, which sprang from a volcanic aquifer. The steam from the hot water left a thick fog that clung to the surface of the water, making it difficult to see more than a few feet ahead. Nobody knew where the river terminated. For that reason, few traversed the river.

To navigate the river, a spirit had to be summoned. It was said that the spirit had a cloak over its head that covered a dark void.

Àjàní, Labí, and Dépò arrived at the bank of Abàmì River before sundown of the first day.

"This is it, warriors—the point of no return," Àjàní declared solemnly.

They dismounted their horses and tied them to a tree.

Àjàní passed Dépò the bull's horn that Fádèyí had given them. "Please, do us the honor."

Dépò took the horn from Àjàní and blew it. Dépò and Labí had fought over Sinmi in the past. He knew that Àjàní was Labí's best friend, but when it came to fighting together or missions, they had to put their differences aside and work together. Otherwise, they could all end up dead. Dépò blew the horn a second time, but nothing happened. He blew it a third time.

They stared into the haze.

A form began to evolve. It was the Abàmì River spirit. True to legend, it was covered in a black cloak and a hood covered its head. The only visible color in the hood was its beady green eyes. It drifted slowly toward the warriors on a canoe. The bony hands of the spirit gripped the oars. The men resolved to show no fear.

Àjàní nodded to Labí, who stepped forward and surveyed the river spirit.

"Spirit of the Abàmì River, we, the warriors of Odùduwà, summon you to take us to the Àìmò Forest."

The spirit nodded and signaled for them to enter the canoe.

In exchange for their passage, Àjàní dropped a cowrie shell into the bony palm of the spirit. The shell made a rattling sound as it spun until it pointed south.

The spirit began to paddle slowly.

The warriors looked at each other somberly as they disappeared into the mist.

CHAPTER 23

The Swamp

The canoe reached the edge of the dark and gloomy forest. The spirit nodded to them and paddled away. The men turned on their lamps. Cackles and screeches echoed around them as they slowly advanced. They walked for half a day before they reached the area where the poisonous plant grew.

Àjàní noticed a movement. He raised his left hand, gesturing for Labí and Dépò to stop.

The warriors stood with spears in their hands, poised for whatever strange phenomenon would accost them.

Àjàní whispered, "Hold very still, warriors." The movement became more aggressive as it got closer. The leaves of the plants and trees shook belligerently. The movement seemed to surround them.

The men remembered their trainings. The men formed an impenetrable triangle with their backs against each other. They dipped their hands into their pouches and brought out some magic powder Fádèyí had given them. They rubbed the powder on their faces, which allowed them to see beyond the physical realm.

They could now see numerous spirits encircling them.

The spirits of the Àìmò Forest moved in on the warriors.

They dipped their hands into their pouches again and retrieved small bottles of magic potions. They sipped them and sprayed them in the air.

Àjàní declared, "You spirits of Àìmò Forest shall do us no harm. You spirits of Àìmò Forest shall allow us to pass—the living do not mingle with the dead!"

The spirits conceded and drifted away from the warriors, revealing a path.

The men stayed close together as they trod down the path. They arrived at a shallow, swampy area with bare trees. The stems and branches resembled skeletons. In the middle of the dry trees, they saw the poisonous plant. The plant's fluorescent green leaves glowed luminously in the dark. No living plant or creature existed in the forest except this one.

"This is it, warriors," Àjàní said.

Labí and Dépò nodded.

"I think one of us should gather the leaves while the other two keep watch," Dépò suggested.

Àjàní shook his head in disagreement. "We should all go. The swamp may be too dangerous for only one person."

"I agree," Labí affirmed.

Dépò was not convinced, but he was outnumbered. They had to work as a unit.

The three brave warriors stepped into the waist-deep water of the swamp. The roots of the trees began to stretch toward them. They were several steps in before they realized what was happening. The brackish water hid the roots until they started to wrap around their ankles. The roots were attempting to pull them underwater.

Àjàní and Dépò pulled out their cutlasses and started to hack at the roots.

Labí drew his cutlass, but he was too late. The branches caught his ankle and pulled him under before he could swing. The force of the pull knocked his cutlass from his hand. It flew into the swamp as the roots dragged him underwater. He grabbed a dagger from his waist and began to blindly cut at the branches that ensnared his ankles. He struggled to breathe.

Àjàní and Dépò saw bubbles and raced toward Labí. They pulled him up and began to slash the branches from his neck and arms. New roots and branches grasped the warriors in an attempt to drown them.

Àjàní opened another potion and poured its contents into the swamp.

The roots and branches began to retract.

Labí and Dépò quickly opened their own bottles and followed suit.

The rest of the foliage recoiled.

The warriors' skills and strength had been tested—and they had just begun their mission. The men breathed heavily as they approached the poisonous plant.

"Let's pluck the seven leaves and get out of this deathly forest," Labí said.

"Yes, but we cannot touch them with our bare hands., Àjàní replied. "Remember what Bàbá Fádèyí said: the leaves are not to touch human skin."

"Then how do we pluck them?" Labí looked around.

Àjàní pulled a small piece of cloth from his bag, wrapped it around his right hand, and plucked seven leaves. He gently dropped them into the bag.

Labí and Dépò glanced furtively around the swamp.

"Let's get out of here, warriors," Àjàní said.

The three men slowly backed away from the plant.

They were nearly out of the swamp when Àjàní exclaimed, "My foot just hit something!"

The three men froze.

Àjàní slowly reached down and pulled out Labí's lost cutlass. "I believe this belongs to you." He handed the cutlass to Labí, smiling.

"Many thanks, my friend." Labí grabbed the cutlass and tucked it back around his waist.

They proceeded cautiously through the darkness. They could only see a few steps ahead.

When they arrived at the edge of the forest, Àjàní raised the bull's horn and blew it three times.

The spirit reappeared in the mist. Its eyes shined a little brighter. No one had ever made it back from the forest alive.

Labí addressed the spirit. "We, the warriors of Odùduwà, summon you, the spirit of the Abàmì River, to take us back to the land of the living."

The spirit nodded.

They entered the canoe and dropped another cowrie shell into the spirit's fleshless hand. Àjàní breathed a sigh of relief as he pushed the canoe away from the shore. The spirit and its human cargo vanished into the dense fog.

CHAPTER 24

The Cave

The spirit paddled the warriors back to the bank of the Abàmì River. The trio had five days left to complete the mission.

They arrived at the riverbank at sunrise of the second day. The next challenge was a long ride across the forests that led to the mouth of the Olúwéré cave. They were to collect three eggs from the ferocious giant lizard that lived there.

Àjàní, Labí, and Dépò retrieved their horses and set off toward the southeast in the direction of the Olúwéré cave. Fatigue was starting to build from the physical exertion and the adrenaline coursing through their veins. It kept them alive, but the many unknowns kept them in a constant state of alert.

The men arrived at the mouth of the cave just as the sun was retiring behind the trees. The darkness of the cave consumed the final rays of daylight. The men secured their horses, grabbed their weapons, and proceeded into the cave.

They gathered bones and rags at the cave entrance and lit torches. The torches illuminated the countless bones of victims who had attempted adventures into the cave in the not-too-distant past. They looked at each other with a glimmer of fear.

"Be careful, warriors," said Àjàní. "I smell death in here."

Labí looked around cautiously and then stated boldly, "No one is dying today. We survived the swamp. We shall survive this cave."

After an hour of walking, Labí stopped, furrowing his brow. "The more we walk, the farther the distance."

"Bring out the pegs from Bàbá Fádèyí," Dépò instructed. "This must be what they are meant for."

Àjàní brought out specially carved, thumb-sized wooden pegs. The insignia of the ifá oracle at the top signified the power they held.

"Put a peg in the ground every ten steps. It shall shrink the distance," Dépò directed.

They inserted the pegs as they moved forward. They soon reached a clearing with fifty-foot stalactites and stalagmites. In another time, they might have admired their beauty, but in the prevailing situation, they seemed ominous.

Neither the giant lizard nor its eggs were in sight. The shadows of the towering structures hid many areas of the cave. The warriors considered the situation.

"I suggest we split up and proceed in these directions." Àjàní pointed three ways, from left to right. "We shall cover this entire area. We shall find the eggs or the lizard one way or another. Call out if you see anything."

Labí and Dépò nodded. They held their torches in front of them as they combed the cave, but they could not find the eggs or the lizard.

As Dépò made his way back from a narrow passage, his foot hit something hard in the soil. He crouched to take a closer look, holding his torch in his right hand. He put down his spear and brushed the soil off an egg. "I think I found something!"

As he observed the dark green eggs, a drop of fluid splattered beside his hand. He looked up at the stalactite above him. Two dark eyes blinked back. The fluids had dropped from the nose of the giant lizard.

The camouflage was perfect. Dépò could not tell the difference between the structures and the giant creature as it hung from above. *The big reptile must have been watching us since we entered the cave.*

The creature took a deep breath and lunged.

Dépò picked up his spear, ducked, and rolled away to avoid the attack.

It was too late. The lizard swung its muscular tail at Dépò. The force of the impact sent him flying through the air.

He crashed against a stalagmite, losing his spear and torch, and was knocked out cold.

Àjàní and Labí raced toward him.

The big lizard moved rapidly toward the unconscious Dépò to finish him off. It opened its mouth, and its long tongue slithered in and out.

Àjàní thrust his spear with all his strength. The spear entered the lizard's jaw, forcing it to draw back.

The big lizard let out an agonizing growl and stared furiously at the men.

The lizard charged toward Àjàní and Labí.

The pair fearlessly moved toward the creature, cutlasses drawn.

The lizard swung its sharp tail toward the two warriors.

Labí ducked to avoid the impact, and Àjàní swung his cutlass with all his might. It collided with the lizard's tail, damaging it severely.

The nimble creature howled and retreated, baiting them to approach.

Labí moved closer to the lizard. "I shall distract it. Go get Dépò's spear," he proposed as he picked up a stone and hurled it at the reptile.

Àjàní grabbed Dépò's spear.

The lizard lunged forward; its salivating mouth opened wide.

Àjàní took a few quick steps to gain momentum and released the spear with all the vigor he could muster.

The weapon pierced the lizard's left eye. It roared in pain. The creature paused and took a breath. Its jaw opened, showing rows of jagged teeth, and prepared to sink them into Labí's skull.

In one swift motion, Labí rolled out of the way and thrust his cutlass into the creature's jaw.

The lizard growled in pain and retreated to the darker part of the cave—with a spear stuck in one eye and a spear and cutlass in its jaw.

Àjàní and Labí had always worked well together, and this incident was no exception. With their torches in hand, Àjàní and Labí held up their remaining weapons to defend themselves if the lizard returned. They helped Dépò up and rested his back against the cave wall. Dépò's stomach had a large, bloody gash. Àjàní and Labí tore some rags, poured liquid from one of their bottles, and placed it on Dépò's cut.

Dépò let out an agonizing scream.

Àjàní and Labí held him down as he regained consciousness.

Dépò was covered in sweat. He opened his eyes and pointed to the eggs nestled in the soil.

"The eggs!" Àjàní exclaimed. He brushed off the soil and dug out an egg. He then saw another and another.

"This lizard is a smart one," Labí said. "It hid all its eggs under the soil."

"Smarter than we think." Àjàní picked out three large eggs, wrapped them in a brown rag, and gently placed them in his sack. "Can you manage, Dépò?"

"I can manage." Dépò clutched his thigh and gut.

Labí grabbed Dépò's torch. "We have to get out of here."

Àjàní helped Dépò limp toward the exit. "Let's go!"

The lizard suddenly reappeared in front of them.

"Keep going! I shall slow it down!" Labí shouted as the lizard drew closer.

Labí swung his spear, but it was not fazed. The creature's good eye blinked at the men.

Àjàní and Dépò rushed toward the entrance of the cave. Àjàní left Dépò at the entrance of the cave and rushed over to the horses. He pulled a bow and arrow from the side of his horse.

Labí turned and ran for the entrance, but he slipped and fell. The lizard was gaining ground. Labí rolled onto his back and looked up at the lizard. It was too late to get up now.

Labí held up his spear and braced himself to meet death.

"A man shall only die once." Labí shut his eyes as the creature lunged forward.

Àjàní's arrow whistled through the air with flawless precision. It hit the lizard right between its eyes, piercing its skull. The lizard crashed to the ground right between Labí's legs.

Labí sat for a moment, stunned. He panted as if he had just run a marathon.

Àjàní held his bow in position. "Labí, let's go!"

Labí jumped to his feet and gave Àjàní a nod of appreciation. It was a close call. He pulled out the spears and cutlass from the lizard's eye, jaw, and skull. He ran toward the exit.

The two best friends looked at each other and burst out laughing. They helped Dépò to his feet and stumbled into the morning breeze.

As they headed toward their horses, Dépò passed out again.

CHAPTER 25

The Forest

"What can we give him?" Àjàní asked.

"Other than the water? We have nothing else." Labí brought a small sack of water to Àjàní.

Àjàní splashed the water on Dépò, which jolted him into consciousness. "What happened?"

"You passed out. You lost a lot of blood," Àjàní replied.

Labí urged, "We have to ride. We must reach the Irúnmolè Forest before nightfall. Dépò, can you manage?"

"I can," Dépò replied weakly.

"Very well. Let's proceed. If you cannot continue, let us know."

Dépò nodded.

Àjàní and Labí helped Dépò onto his horse.

The warriors rode at a steady gallop, only stopping to water the horses. After several hours, they could see the Irúnmolè Forest on the horizon. The sun was bright, but they still had a good distance to cover.

Dépò let out a cry. "I cannot go any farther."

"Hold on," Àjàní said. "We are almost there."

Dépò fell off his horse.

Àjàní and Labí circled back to him.

"Ride with me," Àjàní said.

Dépò shook his head. "I cannot help—not like this. I do not want to slow you down." He let out a rumbling cough. "I'm dead weight. If I come, we all fail."

Àjàní ground his teeth. "Very well... by sundown tomorrow. If you do not see us tomorrow by sundown, get on your horse and ride home. Tell them everything that happened."

They situated Dépò comfortably under a big oak tree. They found some dill plants nearby, made an herbal potion, and gave it to him for healing and strength. They also left him with food and water.

"You shall come back victorious," Dépò proclaimed. "The gods be with you!"

Àjàní and Labí grabbed their weapons and proceeded toward the Irúnmolè Forest. It was starting to get dark.

"Another night mission?" Labí groaned. "I wish we had arrived here earlier. It's even harder navigating these cursed terrains at night."

"We have no choice. Let's make haste," Àjàní replied.

As they disappeared into the foliage, eerie sounds surrounded them. It felt as if they had stepped into another world. Animal sounds echoed from all directions, but there was not an animal in sight.

The men were in search of the Abàmì. These Abàmì creatures had the ability to take different forms, but they mostly roamed the Irúnmolè Forest in their true animal forms. That day, most of the Abàmìs had attended festivals in a nearby village. They took on the form of either masqueraders or guests. Since citizens also attended the festivals in masquerade, one could not easily tell the difference between human and Abàmì. The existence of the Abàmìs was fading into the realm of mythology as they had not been sighted in their true forms for years.

This final mission would test the mettle of the warriors. Fádèyí had instructed the warriors how to approach the spirits without aggravating them, but the men could not avoid this: they were out to steal the skin of an Abàmì. At best, they could only limit the number of Abàmìs they would incite, but a confrontation was inevitable.

The warriors traversed the forest until sunrise, yet they encountered no animals. It was now the fourth day of the mission.

Labí turned to Àjàní. "Remember what Bàbá Fádèyí said about the masquerade festivals working in our favor?"

"I remember. If we hurry, we may get out of here before they get back."

Animal skins lay sprawled on the forest floor. These skins belonged to entities that had transformed into humans on their way to the masquerade festivals. As the warriors passed an animal skin, the animal felt a sense of danger in its human form, wherever it was. The Abàmìs left the festivals in droves and raced back to their skins in the forest. If their skins were destroyed or stolen, they would be trapped in human form until they could generate another skin. Those that could no longer produce a new skin would be trapped in human form for a lifetime.

The fear of being trapped turned the Abàmìs into vicious creatures.

The warriors examined each skin in search of the prized snakeskin. The skin in question belonged to an albino python. She was considered the queen of the Abàmìs. Fádèyí had estimated the skin to be as long as eighteen feet.

The snake was said to live in the trunk of a thousand-year-old Àràbà tree. As big as the tree was, it was said to have flexible branches. The branches could bend from twenty-five meters high to the forest floor. The branches had assumed certain characteristics of the snake queen— or maybe the snake was attracted to the enormous tree because of its branches' snakelike abilities. The warriors would soon find out. They proceeded according to the map Fádèyí had outlined.

In a clearing, one tree stood apart from the others. It was regal. Its branches reached in every possible direction. Its trunk had a large hole, exposing a red interior. The men could see a large heap of animal skins inside.

Labí said, "We cannot tarry here—or the animals shall be upon us."

They examined the skins as quickly as they could, tossing each to the side after inspecting it.

They heard rustling in the foliage.

The Abàmì creatures started to arrive alone or in groups, depending on each animal's social behavior. Some arrived as animals, and some came in human form and transformed in front of the men.

The warriors stared in amazement as the transformations took place right before their eyes. The animals started to growl and hiss. Some retrieved their skins and disappeared into the bushes.

There was a sudden movement in the vegetation. It became more aggressive with every passing second—with louder growls and howls.

Suddenly, hyenas, wild dogs, leopards, and snakes sprang from the bushes toward the men.

The warriors held their cutlasses in one hand and their daggers in the other. They thrust their weapons fiercely, cutting and slicing in all directions.

Àjàní lunged forward and drove his cutlass into one hyena, then pulled it out and swung at a snake.

Labí cut off the heads of two wild dogs in quick succession and surveyed the remaining predators. "There are too many of them!" he cried out. "Let's climb that tree!"

They fought their way to the bottom of the Àràbà tree, caught the closest branches, and climbed as fast as they could.

The animals gathered at the base of the tree and glowered at the men, but they showed no desire to climb. To be safe, the warriors tied themselves to sturdy branches. They were not going to risk falling, which would mean certain death.

Àjàní reached for a branch to pull himself up. His hand brushed something soft and smooth. He touched it again gingerly. It felt cold as he slowly pulled it. It was a dull, yellow snakeskin. "I found it!" he exclaimed.

Àjàní pulled out the entire length of the skin. It stretched at least twelve feet.

"Are you sure this is the skin we need?" Labí asked. King Àjosè's life rested in the warriors' hands. If they presented the wrong sacrifices to the gods, he would surely die.

"What other animal would have skin like this? This is exactly what we need," Àjàní stated confidently. He pulled out the remaining length of skin.

Labí looked down at the animals. "Now if we can just get past these animals."

There was a hissing sound above the men. A massive king cobra slithered toward them and flickered its tongue in the air.

The warriors froze. They could not climb down. The wild animals still lurked at the bottom of the tree.

The king cobra raised its head and came closer. Its neck flattened into a broad hood, exposing a yellow undertone. It arched backward, poised to strike.

Time slowed down for Àjàní. He had seen death many times, but this was different. The menacing black eyes of the cobra held a more treacherous type of death.

The snake bared its fangs.

Àjàní leaned back and swung his cutlass. The last three inches of the cutlass caught the reptile's neck. The force of the assault snapped the branch that held him.

The snake's head flew off and landed on the back of a hyena, not far from the base of the tree. Its fangs sank into the back of the hyena, and the little venom left in its fangs drained into the animal.

The hyena howled and staggered into the forest to find a peaceful place to die.

Àjàní plunged toward the vicious animals below, but the branch held his weight. He stopped a few feet from the forest floor, the branch swinging him back and forth. His back slammed against the tree trunk, and he blacked out. His weapons dropped to the ground as he hung upside down.

The animals moved in for the kill.

"Àjàní!" Labí hurriedly cut the branch that held him. A wild dog lunged toward Àjàní. In that moment, Labí leaped off the tree. The wild dog crashed to the ground as Labí's cutlass connected with its skull, shattering its head. Labí spun off the ground and flipped backward toward Àjàní with his cutlass in one hand and his dagger in the other. He landed on his feet and started cutting and stabbing any animal that dared approach. He stayed as close as possible to Àjàní and cut the branch that held him upside down.

Àjàní hit the forest floor headfirst and jolted back to consciousness.

"*Dìde, dìde!*" (Get up, get up!) Labí grabbed Àjàní.

Àjàní reeled in pain, but there was no time to dwell on it. He grabbed his cutlass and dagger from the ground and joined the fight.

The animals circled, poised to attack, but then they started to retreat. The men looked on in wonder as a woman with red hair and silver eyes emerged from the forest. A gold wrapper flowed from her bosom to her ankles. The pale skin on her neck, arms, and dainty feet was exposed.

All the animals bowed.

She was a sight to behold. She walked gingerly on the balls of her feet. She appeared to barely touch the ground. She swayed in a pronounced sexual manner as she walked toward the men.

The warriors were mesmerized.

She stopped a few feet from the men. "Men of Odùduwà, what brings you to our world?" Her voice sounded like a hiss, and she spoke with a lisp.

The men stood in awe. What a strange beauty. Her long red hair was tied in a braid.

Àjàní nudged Labí. "Don't forget you have Sinmi at home—but I am still available."

"You are on your own with this one, my friend. I certainly shall not be in attendance at your wedding with a snake," Labí replied.

They both chuckled.

She fiddled with the end of her braid and brought out a talisman. Her eyes glowed even brighter as she raised her voice and pointed the talisman at Àjàní. "You have taken what is precious to me!"

A strange wave overcame Àjàní. He dropped to the ground, paralyzed.

CHAPTER 26

Bravery and Death

The mysterious woman was the yellow python in human form. She possessed magical powers.

I don't know if we can withstand this opponent, Labí thought.

"Yes, it would be a waste of time to fight me, humans," the woman said.

She can read thoughts! Labí was startled.

The woman hissed, "You have killed my friends and family—and now you have my skin."

Labí helped Àjàní up from his brief paralysis. Àjàní held his backside. He was still in significant pain. "What if we don't let go of the skin?" he asked.

The woman hissed again, revealing long canine teeth and a slithering tongue. "Very well. You shall die a miserable death!"

The woman let out an unnerving, high-pitched shriek. Venomous snakes emerged from behind her and began slithering along tree trunks, branches, and foliage. They lined up behind the woman, waiting for orders to attack. The snakes were beautiful—each had different markings and exotic color patterns—but this was no time to admire their splendor.

The warriors had never seen such an assortment of snakes.

The woman nodded in the direction of the warriors. The animals moved in, and the carnage commenced.

The warriors swung their cutlasses. Pieces of reptilian flesh flew in all directions. The men were forced to retreat to the bushes. They felt a rattling movement behind them.

Àjàní turned around. A black mamba snake lunged at him and clamped down on his left thigh. It sunk its teeth into his flesh, pumping venom into his veins. He swung his cutlass and cut off the snake's head in one swift motion, but the damage had been done. He fell to the floor as the venom coursed through his body.

The woman raised her hands and yelled, "Ótó! (Enough!)

The snakes and other animals stopped at once.

Labí was covered in blood from the animals and reptiles.

"Now, ask yourselves. Is my skin worth your lives?"

Labí looked at Àjàní lying wounded on the ground. "If we must die here, then so be it." He crouched in a defensive stance and raised his dagger and cutlass, ready to fight to the death.

The snakes moved in to resume their attacks.

"Ótó! Ejòó! (Enough! Please!)

The snakes retreated.

The woman shook her head. "I have never seen such bravery in humans. I shall give you the skin as a parting gift. However, in exchange, you humans must let us live in peace. Now that you know we still exist, let others be mindful of it. You must not return to our world to violate us again. Next time, we shall not be so gracious." She looked at the snakes and raised her hand. "Let them pass."

The snakes retreated.

Labí helped Àjàní up. They sheathed their cutlasses and daggers and fastened their spears to their backs.

"We are thankful," Labí said, bowing in gratitude.

They made their way through the gap, but Àjàní started to slip into unconsciousness.

Labí reached into his sack and brought out the antivenom from Fádèyí.

The ifá oracle had revealed all these challenges to Fádèyí, and he had prepared them well for it. However, the outcome of the mission had not been revealed to him. Labí poured the antivenom into Àjàní's mouth, but the poison had already taken effect.

The woman roared, "Your friend shall not live. The poison is in his blood. His life shall not be spared—"

"He shall!" Labí glared at the woman.

"Go before I change my mind," the woman hissed menacingly.

They left the forest at sunset of the fifth day of the mission.

Àjàní grew weaker with every step.

I hope Dépò is still alive, Labí thought. *He could help me keep Àjàní alive.* Labí could not carry Àjàní on his own, but he would rather die in the forest than abandon his best friend.

Àjàní stumbled once more. "Labí, I cannot walk any longer. Please go on without me."

"I shall never do that. Never!"

"I know you'll never agree, you stubborn bastard." Àjàní smiled. He coughed up blood. "But you cannot drag me and make it back home on time."

"Watch me," Labí replied, refusing to accept his comrade's demise.

"Very well, then. You go ahead. I shall rest here then catch up with you."

"Shut up!" Labí shouted as tears welled up his eyes. He picked up Àjàní and spread him across his shoulders. "I am tying the knot with Sinmi soon. You vowed to be by my side on that day." He was not leaving his best friend behind.

Àjàní forced a smile. "My presence shall surely be felt on that day. We shall drink wine together."

Labí carried Àjàní on his shoulders for miles. He could barely see in the dark. They had lost their torches during their encounter with the Abàmì creatures. Death seemed to hang in the still, humid air.

It was sundown of the following day. They made it to the edge of the forest, not far from where they had left Dépò. Labí's knees gave out. He too was weak and was becoming delirious.

Labí spotted a small fire on the other side of the forest. *I hope it's Dépò.* He was their only hope. "Dépò! Dépò! Dépò!" Labí hoped his voice would echo, but the wind was still. He shouted for a short while, but he soon became too weak to yell. "Àjàní, I too cannot continue any farther. We have given it our best. May the gods have mercy on Odùduwà and us." Labí collapsed in the grass.

Àjàní made no sound.

There was a faint human sound in the distance.

"Àjàní! Labí! Àjàní!"

Labí sat up.

It was getting louder.

"Dépò!" Labí called.

"Àjàní! Labí!"

"Dépò!"

There was a glimmer of hope. Dépò was alive.

"I thought you were dead!" Labí cried out.

"I'm still here. And I see you are, too," he remarked with a slight smile.

Dépò was still in pain after the lizard attack, but he had regained strength from the herbal potion the warriors had prepared. "You know I can't die," he said wryly.

The warriors laughed and embraced.

"We can't proceed in this condition. We should wait until morning," Dépò said.

"I agree," said Labí. "I am weak, and Àjàní needs to rest. We shall rest until morning and then ride fast to make it on time for the sacrifice."

"Labí!"

Labí awoke with a start. At first, he thought it was a dream, but he heard his name again as clear as day.

Àjàní tried to raise his hand to signal to Labí.

It was early morning, and the sun had not yet risen. Àjàní called out to him, and Labí rushed to Àjàní's side.

Àjàní looked up with a weak smile. "See? I'm still here."

"Yes, you are, my friend. Yes, you are." Labí was happy to see his friend alive.

"Tell my father I'm sorry I won't be hunting with him next season." Tears rolled down Labí and Dépò's faces. The brave warrior was slipping away.

"It was an honor fighting beside you warriors. Make sure Odùduwà never forgets me. Tell them about our bravery."

"You shall tell your kids and grandkids yourself—you shall make it!" Labí shook his head. He was not ready to see his companion die.

Àjàní smiled weakly. "I am the cat with nine lives, but the last one has been spent. No one survives a mamba attack like this." He grabbed Labí's arm. "Tell the people of my bravery. Promise?"

Labí could not respond. He sobbed uncontrollably.

"And who knows? I may become an oracle and protect you from beyond."

Dépò said, "Àjàní, we promise. We shall tell of your bravery. We shall make you a legend, and we shall have a statue erected in your honor."

Àjàní mumbled a few more words and stopped. His eyes remained open, but his stare became blank. His eyes stopped moving. A distant object had permanently caught his attention. Àjàní was dead.

Labí held on, hunched over his friend. "Àjàní, I'm listening. You said we should make you great. I promise. Just stay with us. Let us get you home. Àjàní, Àjàní!"

"Labí, he has gone to the great beyond." Dépò patted Labí's shoulder and closed Àjàní's eyes.

Labí let out a long, anguished scream.

Dépò pried Àjàní's body from Labí's grip. "We must resume our journey immediately; otherwise, we may miss the sacrifice, and his death shall be for nothing."

Labí refused to move.

Dépò grabbed Labí's arm. "Get up, warrior! We must go. Be strong."

They placed Àjàní's body on his horse and secured him tightly.

Labí continued to sob as he mounted his own horse.

It was the sixth day. The sacrifice had to be offered the following day. The chiefs and elders anxiously awaited the warriors' arrival.

The royal family, the elders, and the Odùduwà warriors had gathered in the main square. They sang songs to maintain morale. At twilight on the sixth day, the warriors appeared on the horizon. Only two horses carried warriors; the third horse had something draped over it that resembled a large sack.

Labí and Dépò reached the center of the square. Their faces and bodies were still covered with blood. They led Àjàní's horse through the crowd with his body across it. They stopped in front of Àjàmú and Sóbógun, the second-in-command, and dismounted. They reverently placed Àjàní's body at Àjàmú's feet.

Àjàmú had accepted the possibility of death when the warriors started the mission, but nothing could have prepared him to see his son's dead body. "Ah! Àjàníogun, my son! What a great warrior you were. How I wish I could take your place. My son, my son!" Àjàmú was not one to show emotion, but he could not control himself this time. His whole body shook with grief as tears tumbled down his face.

Sóbógun also shed tears but remained stoic, steadying Àjàmú with his muscular arms.

Fádèyí bowed his head in sorrow.

Wails erupted from some of the warriors.

Labí bellowed, "Àjàní's last wish was that we would not forget him. He was a great warrior of Odùduwà. Now, warriors and citizens of Odùduwà, honor him!"

Several warriors rushed forward. They lined up in perfect sequence and picked up Àjàní's body. The rest stood to show respect for the dead warrior.

Labí and Dépò turned and bowed in front of the queen.

"We have gathered the items required for the sacrifice. We have returned with everything but Àjàní's life." Labí dropped the brown sack in front of the queen.

Queen Adélolá had no words as tears streamed down her face.

CHAPTER 27

The Sacrifice

The next morning, the mood was solemn in Odùduwà. Àjàní's corpse was being prepared. It would be washed and oiled to preserve it for several days if necessary. The oils that had soaked into the dead flesh would produce a pleasant aroma when the body was cremated. It was said that the aroma was to please the gods and induce them to welcome the spirit of the departed.

Queen Adélolá supervised the preparation of the body.

A great warrior had just fallen, but it was also the seventh day—the day of the sacrifice. It was tradition that no one in the land could leave their home on the day that a sacrifice was being prepared and carried to its destination. If anyone saw the act, it was believed that person would take on the curse being exorcized. Such a person could be exiled or put to death without question.

Fádèyí took the bag with the items for the sacrifice and headed toward the king's chamber.

Dòngárì stepped aside as the chief priest entered the king's room.

Fádèyí placed the seven poisonous leaves, the three eggs, and the python's skin beside the king. He started to chant as he rubbed the poisonous leaves on the king's feet and then placed them in a wooden mortar beside him. He took the eggs, touched the king's head, shoulders, arms and feet, and placed them in the wooden mortar.

He took the python's skin and stretched it over the king's body. He chanted as he made patterns in the air above the king's body, and then he placed the skin in the mortar too. He added dried pepper, palm oil, and other items. He called for a maid to bring a freshly slaughtered rooster and drained the blood into the mortar. He took a small wooden pestle and ground everything together. He scraped the contents in an open calabash. "Dòngárì!"

Dòngárì entered the room.

"Please summon three warriors. We are heading to Odò Ọba at once."

Dòngárì nodded and rode off.

Queen Adélọlá entered with her baby in her arms. "How is the preparation coming, Bàbá Fádèyí?"

"The sacrifice is ready," Fádèyí replied.

The baby let out a cry.

Queen Adélọlá rocked the little prince to pacify him. "What are we waiting for?"

"I have sent for three warriors, Your Highness. We shall commence the moment they arrive," Fádèyí replied.

"Thank you, Bàbá Fádèyí." Queen Adélọlá looked at the king and called one of her maids. "Àpèké!"

Àpèké entered the king's chamber. "Your Highness?"

The queen handed the prince to the maid.

Dòngárì arrived with the three warriors, and they dismounted and knelt on one knee before the queen.

"Ah! They are here. Now we shall commence," Bàbá Fádèyí said as he stood up.

"Your Highness," the warriors greeted.

"Please stand." The queen smiled. "Thank you, warriors of Odùduwà, for your loyalties. May the gods be with you as you go."

The warriors nodded. "Àsheee."

"May our ancestors also go with us," Bàbá Fádèyí added.

"Àsheee!" the warriors said.

"Warriors, leave your horses behind. You shall have no need for them. We shall walk."

"We are ready," the men replied.

Bàbá Fádèyí mumbled some incantations and touched the warriors' foreheads one after another to protect them from any curse. When he was finished, he picked up the sacrifice and placed it in the hands of one of the warriors. He also picked up his staff and a white horsetail. He waved it continuously as he led the way to the Ọba River.

They arrived at the Ọba River at noon.

Bàbá Fádèyí turned to the warrior who was carrying the sacrifice. "Jagunmólú, place the sacrifice down there." He pointed to a shallow area of the river.

Jagunmólú nodded and entered the Ọba River. When he was knee-deep in the river, he placed the sacrifice on the surface.

They all watched as the current carried the sacrifice down the river.

Fádèyí raised his staff in excitement. "The sacrifice has been accepted! Jagunmólú, you may return to land."

Jagunmólú started heading back to shore. Suddenly, a powerful force pulled him under the water.

Fádèyí raised his hands in protest. His white tunic dropped to the floor, exposing his traditional black undergarment, which was decorated with cowrie shells that had magical powers. He raised his staff and yelled, "*Èèwò! A ò kí ń fi ọmọ orè bo rè! Óyá! Dáa padà! Mo ní kí e dáa padà, eléèyí kìí se eran ìje! E dáa padà kíá!*" (Sacrilege! It is forbidden to sacrifice the children of the gods to the gods! Return him now! I say! Return him now! This one is not part of the sacrifice. Return him now!)

The warriors looked on anxiously. They had never seen Bàbá Fádèyí act this way. The radiation that flowed from him was so powerful that smoke emerged from his staff. Fádèyí plunged his staff into the water and continued to chant.

A strange thing occurred. A wall of water formed about a mile down the river. It held for several minutes, and then it began pushing the water back upstream.

The warriors stared as the direction of the current reversed. Moments later, Jagunmólú's body appeared, bouncing in the current.

The two warriors pulled him out of the water and tried to revive him.

Bàbá Fádèyí knelt beside Jagunmólú and held his head. *"Omo owó kìí kú lójú owó. Omo esè kìí kú lójú esè, Jagunmólú! Dìde kìà!* (It is impossible for an infant child to die without justification. It is impossible for an adult to die without reason. Jagunmólú! Get up now!)

Jagunmólú coughed up water and opened his eyes.

Fádèyí picked up his tunic and wrapped it around his waist.

The two warriors helped Jagunmólú up. The party rushed back to the palace.

The queen sat beside King Àjosè, waiting for Bàbá Fádèyí to bring her good news. She felt a touch on her side. It was Àjosè's hand. She breathed a sigh of relief. The queen looked up and gave thanks to the gods.

CHAPTER 28

Farewell

"I'm famished," the king said.

Queen Adélolá called to her maids. "Bring me a cup of water!"

A maid brought a cup and handed it to the queen.

As Àjosè was about to take a sip, Fádèyí and his entourage entered. "*Dúró!*" (Stop!) he yelled.

The queen paused, confused. "But the king is thirsty, Bàbá Fádèyí."

"He must drink this first." Fádèyí produced a liquid potion in a small bottle.

"Very well, Bàbá Fádèyí." Queen Adélolá helped the king consume the potion.

Àjosè sat up and glanced around the room, puzzled. "What happened? How long have I been here? What day is it?"

Fádèyí replied, "You have been bedridden for seven days now, Your Highness."

Kúyè bowed. "Welcome back, Your Highness."

The queen added, "Yes, my king. And that wicked King Guguwa is in the dungeon."

"What have you done? Why is he down there?" King Àjosè asked.

"He was the last person you touched before you fell unconscious. All precautions needed to be taken, Your Highness," Kúyè replied.

The king turned to Fádèyí. "What do you make of this, Bàbá?"

Fádèyí looked at the queen and Kúyè, and then he looked back at King Àjosè. He wanted to explain without offending the queen, but being a man of integrity, he had to tell the truth. "King Guguwa of Hawani was just a victim of circumstance, Your Highness. He was simply at the wrong place at the wrong time. The king of Hawani had nothing to do with your ailment. This was provoked by the gods."

"And have we appeased them?" Àjosè asked.

"For now," Fádèyí replied. "In due time, the gods shall reveal the entire picture." Bàbá Fádèyí told the king about the warriors' mission and all that had happened, including the death of Àjàní, the general's son.

Àjosè stood with the help of two guards. He was both furious and grief-stricken. He tore at his garments. "Kúyè, bring King Guguwa to me at once. Bring Àjàmú as well!" He staggered out of the room, heading to the king's court.

"Yes, my king." Kúyè hurried off to the dungeon with some guards.

The queen followed the king and steadied him with her arm. "My love, you are not recovered enough to make judgments."

The king ignored her plea. The thought of all the sacrifices required to save his life infuriated him. "Some matters need urgent attention, Adélolá, and this is one of them!"

Down in the dungeon, King Guguwa fumed as he sat on the rough stone slab in his cell. *King Àjosè and his wicked witch shall pay for this!*

Accompanied by Kúyè, the guards brought King Guguwa to the court.

Servants came and put new garments on King Àjosè as he sat on his throne.

"Unchain him now!" King Àjosè demanded.

The guards took off the chains, and Guguwa knelt in respect. "I have said unpleasant things in the past, but I had nothing to do with your ailment at the ceremony, my lord. I promise you this."

Àjosè leaned forward. "Please stand. I believe you, and I apologize for what you have endured as a result. I hope you can understand that necessary precautions needed to be taken. I truly hope this does not drive a wedge between us."

"I understand, Your Highness. No apology is needed." King Guguwa forced a smile.

King Àjosè walked over to King Guguwa and held out his hand. "Thank you for your understanding. Go home in peace."

Guguwa was clothed in expensive garments and sent home with escorts and costly gifts to appease him, but none of this could soothe his hurt pride. After being disrespected and humiliated, he had revenge on his mind. However, he hid his feelings and pretended he was in a good mood as he left Odùduwà.

King Àjosè remained in the court, alone with his thoughts. *Why are things going so wrong in my era?*

Queen Adélolá walked in. "Your Highness, you must rest now. You have been through a great ordeal."

The king shook his head. "How can I rest after all that has happened? Àjàmú's son lost his life because of me. How do I right this wrong, Lolá?"

The queen nodded empathetically. "This is the way of the warrior, my king."

"I know, Lolá, but he was the general's son."

A guard knocked on the door. "May I approach, Your Highness?"

"Come in," Àjosè replied.

The guard approached the king and whispered in his ear.

"Ah! Please let him in," the king said.

Àjàmú entered the court and bowed. "My queen."

"General," Queen Adélolá responded.

Àjàmú knelt on one knee before the king. "My king."

Àjosè moved toward Àjàmú. "My dear friend, please rise." He held out his hands.

Adélolá would let them have their moment. "Good to see you again, General. I am so sorry for your loss. It is a great loss to us all. I shall leave you two to speak. Please allow me to put the prince to bed."

After the queen left, King Àjosè turned solemnly to Àjàmú. "How can I make it up to you, my dear friend?"

"There is nothing to make up for, my king. The mission needed to be carried out." Àjàmú took a deep breath. "He died doing what he loved—what he was born to do. I am glad you are alive."

"He shall have a burial befitting the great warrior that he was," King Àjosè said.

"Thank you, my king. He shall be sent off to our ancestors three days from today," Àjàmú said.

"Very well. Anything you need, my friend," emphasized King Àjosè.

On the third day after the sacrifice, the warriors of Odùduwà gathered in the city square.

Àjàmú's heart pounded as he looked down at his son's lifeless body. He placed two cowrie shells on his eyes. "Àjàní, my son, I never envisioned this day would occur in my lifetime. You have been a great warrior since you were a boy. You always wanted everything done to perfection. I thought I was going to beat you to this one." He smiled forlornly. "But like everything else, you have beaten me to this too. Sooner or later, I shall catch up to you. Farewell, my son."

Labí and Dépò could not hold back their tears.

King Àjosè and Queen Adélolá stood opposite Àjàmú at the foot of the wooden pyre, and Elder Kúyè stood behind them.

King Àjosè addressed the crowd. "People of Odùduwà, I thank you for all you have done while I was indisposed. A great warrior has given his life for me. I am filled with sorrow over this loss and all that has happened. As Àjàní gave his life for me, I would give my life for each and every one of you. We are sending our son to the great beyond—to rest with our ancestors. May the gods receive his spirit."

"Àsheee," the people responded.

King Àjosè raised his scepter to signal the beginning of the cremation.

Àjàmú, King Àjosè, members of the royal guard, and close family were given torches.

Àjàmú lit his torch, walked over to Àjàní's body, and kissed his forehead. "Rest in peace and power, my son." He set fire to the pyre.

King Àjosè and the others lit their torches and added to the flames.

The town crier proclaimed, "There shall be seven days of mourning. Everyone must put on a sackcloth."

The crowd dispersed quietly, but Àjàmú stayed with Àjosè and a few close friends and warriors.

Labí and Dépò stood behind Àjàmú and watched the flames as their friend's body was consumed. A cloud of smoke formed above the pyre. It looked like a face—Àjàní's face. A few moments later, it rose into the clouds. Those who were watching caught the form.

"Àjàní has departed us," Fádèyí confirmed.

King Àjosè put his hand on Àjàmú's shoulder. "Let us go home, my friend."

Àjàmú walked beside the king, his eyes downcast. He choked back tears. Labí, Dépò, and the rest of the warriors followed them. The thick smoke continued to rise into the clouds.

CHAPTER 29

Deliberating Fate

Àmínù the Madawaki, the general of the Hawani kingdom army, strode into the palace and glared at the queen of Hawani. "What happened in Odùduwà?"

Garzo, the head of the elders, held up his hand. "This is your queen. Your insolence shall not be tolerated."

Àmínù turned to Garzo. "Perhaps you have answers, then! Where is the king?"

The arrival of the queen of Hawani without the king had caused an uproar in the kingdom of Hawani. She had arrived in the middle of the night. The disheveled queen perched on her throne without the king raised questions.

It was the first day of the month. The king was expected to oversee the allocation of resources and assignments on the first day of every month. Hawani was a commercial hub, intersecting the trade routes of North Africa and the coast. Without his approval, certain aspects of the kingdom's day-to-day life would come to a grinding halt.

Garzo approached the queen. "My queen, can you tell us where the king is?"

"He is in a dungeon in Odùduwà," the queen replied in a defeated tone.

"The king is in a dungeon in Odùduwà—and you are here?" Àmínù the Madawaki asked incredulously.

Garzo stepped between Àmínù and the queen. "You shall shut your mouth, Àmínù! If you dare to challenge tradition that existed before your father was born, you shall be stripped of everything of value."

The queen did not have much authority herself, but protocol was strictly adhered to in Hawani. It was not the place of the military officers to engage the queen; they were beneath her. But the absence of the king had thrown the court into confusion, and the chain of command had been blurred.

The queen recounted the events that led to King Guguwa being thrown into the dungeon. "I had no choice but to leave. Someone had to bring the news home."

Dambo, an elder, interjected. "What shall happen to His Highness now?" He was an impatient man and rarely thought before he spoke.

Tears welled up in the queen's eyes. "I do not know. King Àjosè is in a coma. If he dies, they may put my husband to death."

Dambo moved closer to the queen. "They would not dare. We shall dispatch warriors at once."

Tanko, another elder, piped up and said, "There is no need to panic. I am sure we shall get to the bottom of—"

"This is not the time for diplomacy, Elder Tanko," Àmínù interrupted. "While we are talking, our king may be killed."

"We cannot make rash decisions," Tanko countered. "We do not know the full story. And Odùduwà is the dominant empire in this region. To take them on, we need allies. And it would be hard to gather allies, especially from kingdoms loyal to Odùduwà or under its control. I suggest we send emissaries, not warriors, to Odùduwà."

King Guguwa rode slowly toward Hawani on his horse. The tropical rain forest of Odùduwà was giving way to the middle savannas, and the air was becoming drier and familiar. He felt like he could breathe again. He mused on the events of the past few days. *Very unfortunate*, he thought. *I was starting to have some regard for Àjosè. Even though he rules the dominant kingdom in the region, I deserve more respect than I received. Hawani used to be the powerhouse of the region. We were the gate of trade with kingdoms in the far north and the Persians—even as far as the Orient. To be wrongly accused of poisoning the king in front of the dignitaries and thrown in a dungeon? If I had desired so, I could have planned a much better way to assassinate him!* He shook his head. *My ancestors shall be turning in their graves.*

"Your Royal Highness, are we almost there?" asked one of his escorts.

Guguwa looked back at the two servants Àjosè had assigned him to carry the gifts. *These ones even have the audacity to ask me questions.*

"We did not hear, Your Highness. We are wondering if we are almost there."

"We'll be there soon. We have less than a day. Stop talking and ride." King Guguwa continued forward. He shook his head. *I shall accommodate these servants for now lest they kill me in the forest. Riding with only two servants to attend to me is an insult.*

The servants whispered as they rode along.

"I do not care much for him," one servant said.

"I do not care for this mission either," the other servant responded, "but we were ordered to carry these gifts and wait on him."

"I wish we had warriors with us. He is known for his treacherous ways."

After another kilometer, King Guguwa and the servants stopped. A cloud of dust billowed in the distance. Sandstorms were common in the region.

The cloud grew bigger, and figures started to emerge. Six men with turbans and white kaftans quickly approached them on horses. As they drew closer, the flag of the Hawani kingdom became visible.

King Guguwa raised his hand. The riders jumped off their horses and bowed.

"O King, we heard you had been thrown into a dungeon in Odùduwà, and that they were prepared to kill you. The gods be praised—we have our king back!"

"Enough, enough! Let us go home," King Guguwa asserted.

"Who are these, Your Highness?"

"King Àjosè sent them with me as escorts. They shall come with us," Guguwa replied flatly.

The party of nine rode back to Hawani.

Upon arrival at the city gate, shouts of joy rang out. Royal horns were sounded, and people emerged from their homes to meet the king.

The queen ran out to greet Guguwa, along with the lesser wives. King Guguwa had a harem that would put many a king to shame. He had wives and concubines from many kingdoms, including the Fulani women who were considered some of the most beautiful women in the world.

The king dismounted his horse at the palace entrance.

News had spread quickly. The elders and ministers were waiting for the king. The emissaries and servants followed the king, his advisers, and elders into the palace.

King Guguwa took his place on his throne and faced the crowd. "I thank you, faithful people of Hawani, for your support. I see that news of the events in Odùduwà has proliferated through the kingdom." He looked around. "Our kingdom has been loyal to the Odùduwà kingdom, and we have considered them allies. We have let them dictate the trends in this region, but the time has come to revisit that arrangement. I believe you all have heard how I was treated—thrown into their dungeon, disregarded by the queen, and threatened—only to be told it was a mistake!"

Shouts rose from the crowd.

"Kai."

"They dared!"

"Impossible."

"Yes, my people. I, your king, shall never lie to you. I am telling you the truth."

The crowd hung on his every word.

"We shall teach Odùduwà a lesson. Àjosè shall pay for his crimes against us."

The crowd started to cheer.

"We shall annihilate them!"

"Yes, yes!"

The servants from Odùduwà stared at each other helplessly.

"This is very bad. Things may not end well for us here," one whispered to the other.

King Guguwa raised his hand to quiet the crowd.

"We shall show them!"

"If I may speak, Your Highness?" one servant from Odùduwà spoke up.

Guguwa stopped and looked at the servant in astonishment. "If you may speak?" The king looked at his advisers. "The vermin want to speak. Imagine the insolence."

"Let us allow him to speak," Garzo said.

Everyone turned to the duo from Odùduwà.

"We are citizens of the great kingdom of Odùduwà, but we are the lowest among you. Our only duty is to serve at your behest, and we are loyal to you. We speak only because there is no other voice of higher stature to address this great gathering. We ask that you do not take our address as insolence. Our kingdom—and indeed our king—has faced many unfortunate events in recent times. The most unfortunate event has been to blame you for the ailment of our king. O great King Guguwa, of the even greater Hawani kingdom, we beseech you to show our kingdom mercy."

"He speaks as a lord, this lowly servant," Dambo said.

"They are known for their education and enlightenment," said Garzo.

Tanko nodded. "Even their commoners have impressive knowledge and understanding."

The servant continued, "We were sent to accompany Your Highness to ensure your comfort and safety on the journey home and to ensure all was well before we returned. We are confident, beyond all reasonable doubt, that our king is an honorable man. He shall do all that is necessary to right this wrong accusation and the acts done against you, o dear King. If you shall only give him a chance, Your Highness. We shall carry any message you wish to send back to our king. We beg you and your great people. Just as our king sent us forth with gifts, I am sure he shall do even more to assuage this justifiable discontent, o great King." He looked around. "We ask that you give peace a chance, Your Highness."

King Guguwa lowered his voice. He looked around the court as he spoke. "He who defecates inside a calabash does not remember the act like he who cleans it up. For many days, I wallowed in a dungeon. I, King Guguwa, received treatment that has never been meted out to any of my predecessors. I was demeaned and disgraced by Odùduwà. My honor was trampled upon, and of all people, by the queen and her adviser, Kúkè or Kukoo—or whatever his name is." King Guguwa looked down at the escorts. "And now, to be addressed by servants of Odùduwà? This is too much. Now, they want peace after they threatened to take my life. They want peace?" King Guguwa looked up suddenly. "Take them to the dungeons."

Three warriors jumped on the servants.

"Take them away from my sight. To the dungeons!" The king collapsed in his chair and turned to the queen. "Have them prepare a bath for me. I must rid myself of the stench of Odùduwà."

The queen got up and clapped her hands.

Two of the king's wives and two concubines followed her to the inner room.

The queen knew what the king fancied. She whispered instructions to the women.

Garzo, the head of the elders, asked, "O great one, what shall we do with the servants?"

"Tomorrow we shall pronounce judgment on them," the king replied. He turned to the people. "I shall ensure that no kingdom ever again treats us with such contempt."

Shouts of celebration erupted from the crowd. Citizens broke into song and dance. The people of Hawani were eager to show Odùduwà that they too were a great people.

CHAPTER 30

The Message

The three elders stepped away from the crowd.

Garzo began, "Odùduwà's treatment of our king was terrible, but the servants made a humble plea for peace. I believe they spoke the truth."

"So, you support what was done to our king?" asked Dambo.

"No, Dambo, but—"

"If we do not send a strong message, imagine what may befall others from our kingdom at the hands of Odùduwà. We should make an example of King Àjosè," declared Dambo.

"And how do you propose we do that?" Garzo asked. "Odùduwà is a great nation, greater than ours. Their army is ruthless."

"They were ruthless because we did not have a cavalry in the past. With the horses we now have from Arabia, they do not stand a chance!" replied Dambo.

"You are being optimistic. I would advise we proceed with caution," Garzo answered steadily.

Tanko chimed in, "My friends, the die is cast. The king has whipped the people into a frenzy, and he seeks blood. He has long coveted the

position of King Àjosè. I do not believe we have much of a choice but
to agree with the king."

The next morning, King Guguwa awoke with renewed drive.
His bath had been satisfying. The queen had overseen the wives and
concubines as they bathed him. She knew what gave him pleasure.
After his morning meal, he called on his political and military leaders.

"This morning shall be momentous. It shall mark the beginning of
the repositioning of Hawani. On this day, we shall take back our glory
from Odùduwà and all other enemies. We shall show our detractors
that we are a force to be reckoned with. What say you of the situation
with Odùduwà?"

The elders had debated through the night. Many of them believed
that King Guguwa should exercise caution, but they knew the king.
Which of them dared to disagree and risk their life? He was asking
for advice, but in his current frame of mind, he was looking for an
agreement. They looked at one another to see which of them would
bell the cat.

Dambo finally spoke up. "I agree with your position, my king.
The disrespect of Odùduwà has reached a climax. We must send a
message to Odùduwà and the surrounding kingdoms that they have
committed a grave error. We must ensure there shall not be a repeat
of such events."

Other elders shook their heads quietly. There was no turning back.

"We must take our rightful place in the region!" Dambo proclaimed.

"Well said, wise man," King Guguwa affirmed.

Garzo hesitated, then spoke up. "O King, if I may give an alternative
view. I suggest we send a message to Odùduwà about the gravity of the
situation and wait to see their response. Perhaps, after the initial apology
and gifts, we may be able to extract more from King Àjosè and position
ourselves without direct conflict."

Everyone went quiet.

The king stared menacingly at Garzo. "You want me to forget what happened and retract into a shell. Do you see me as such a king? Is this the type of leader you want?"

Garzo replied quietly, "No, my king. I am only saying we should consider all options before making a decision."

Other elders murmured in agreement, but they did not speak up.

The king declared, "We shall meet again at sundown, and we shall send a message to Odùduwà!" He stormed out of the court.

The elders looked at one another, unsure of the king's intent.

Evening came, and the gathering reconvened. This time, Àmínù the Madawaki, the warriors, and members of the public were present.

The king sat on his throne. "I thank you, the great people of Hawani, for all you have endured in the past few years. I thank you for enduring the oppression of others. I am here to inform you that our kingdom shall once again take its rightful place among the league of nations. We shall start by addressing the misconduct of Odùduwà." He turned to his guards. "Bring the prisoners."

The guards retrieved the prisoners from the dungeon and brought them before the king.

"Tonight, I shall send a message to Odùduwà through you," King Guguwa said.

The two servants from Odùduwà looked at each other with hope. *Finally, we are going home—away from this godforsaken place.* The heat in the dungeon was unbearable, and the fresh air was a relief.

Guguwa turned to his people and said, "We shall send them back to Odùduwà—but without their bodies!" He turned to Àmínù, the head of his army. "Bring me their heads!"

Àmínù nodded and signaled to the warriors. "Take them away and bring me their heads."

Two warriors grabbed the servants and dragged them to the square outside the palace.

The king and the crowd followed the warriors and the servants to the chopping block.

Garzo and Tanko shook their heads. This was not the best course of action, but they had no choice in the matter.

The men's heads were placed on the chopping block. They were stripped of most of their clothes. The helpless victims could feel the cool breeze of the evening blowing against their bodies. The sunset was beautiful, but all they could see was the soil, thirsty for their blood.

The first servant looked at the second. "My friend, it has been an honor to serve with you. I shall see you on the other side."

The second servant trembled, a solemn look on his face. "We shall meet our ancestors tonight."

The head of the army raised his arm and looked at the king.

The king nodded. The general dropped his arm, and the headsmen brought down the blades with force.

The first servant closed his eyes and prayed as the blade came down. The second servant shrieked in terror.

The scream was cut short as both heads were severed, but it lingered in the air for several seconds. Their eyes remained eerily wide as their bloody heads rolled off the platform and into the hands of two guards.

Guguwa gloated over his display of power. "Put the heads in a sack and send them to Àjosè while they are still fresh. Write a note to the king and tell him to expect retribution from the kingdom of Hawani." He turned to the general. "You know what to do."

The general nodded. "I shall gather the warriors for training immediately, my king." He turned to his high-ranking warriors. "Go into the villages, recruit strong, able-bodied young men, and bring them to me. We shall train them for war. We need all the hands we can get."

"Yes, my lord." The warriors rode off on their horses.

The crowd slowly dispersed as the bodies were collected. The excitement would keep the people going for days.

The king turned to the queen. "I am tense from the day. I shall need a massage tonight. Get the oils I brought back from Odùduwà."

"Yes, Your Highness," the queen replied dutifully.

By the next morning, Àmínù the Madawaki had assembled a group of three messengers and eight warriors to deliver the message to Odùduwà.

Elder Garzo approached the general in the courtyard as he was preparing the group. He gently placed his hand on the general's shoulder. "Do you think the king has taken the correct course of action? This may lead to war. I believe our king should have exercised caution."

Àmínù the Madawaki glared at the elder's hand on his shoulder.

Garzo quickly removed his hand.

"What is done is done," stated the general flatly. "I stand by the king. Are you saying the message should not be delivered?"

"I am saying nothing of the sort. I simply suggest we exercise caution."

Àmínù laughed. "Old man, the heads are off the bodies already. We cannot reattach them and offer the king a different course of action. What is done is done. All of Hawani's enemies shall be taught a lesson." He loaded the heads onto the lead messenger's horse and handed him a cowskin note with markings. "Deliver the heads and this note to King Àjosè." He turned to the warriors. "Defend yourselves if you must." He slapped the rump of the horse.

The horse broke into a gallop. The eight warriors and two remaining messengers followed. Blood seeped from the sacks on the lead horse and dripped down the horse's legs.

Garzo stared ruefully as the group rode away. "There goes the peace of the nation."

CHAPTER 31

A Bad Omen

The group from Hawani rode all day. As evening approached, they slowed down. Odùduwà was still a full day's journey away. The entourage stopped when they reached the tropical rain forests that hosted Odùduwà.

"Let us spend the night here," directed the lead warrior. "The horses need to rest, and I prefer to travel during the day. You never know what you may encounter at night."

The party set up a campfire as the sun went down.

A vulture appeared in the sky, circled the camp three times, and landed on a nearby rock.

One of the messengers stared at the vulture in fear.

The lead warrior shouted, "What are you staring at? Come help us pitch these tents."

The trembling servant pointed at the vulture. "That vulture flew around us three times before it landed. If a vulture does that, it is a sign of death. Now it is staring at us. This is a bad omen."

"You believe in old wives' tales?" the lead warrior mocked. He picked a stone, pushed the servant aside, and hurled it at the bird.

The stone barely missed the vulture, but it was enough to send it squawking into the sky.

The warrior scowled at the messenger. "Now help us set up this tent."

The group settled in their respective tents, each man alone with his thoughts. They were not much for conversation. Outside the camp, darkness took absolute control. The crickets were the only sounds reminding them of life.

The messengers huddled together in the same tent. Two warriors slept in each tent. To them, it was just another mission. They were more concerned with how the message and the servants' heads would be received once they got to Odùduwà. They deliberated among themselves about how to handle potential scenarios. Two of the warriors sat near the fire, keeping watch.

In the middle of the night, a slithering form crawled out from under a rock. The warmth of the fire and the possibility of food in the camp had attracted the puff adder. It had rarely encountered humans so close and was curious. It slid into the tent and stuck out its tongue to taste the air. It listened to the snores of the people. The snake contemplated whether there was anything of interest in the tent.

One of the messengers turned over and stretched out his arm.

The sudden movement startled the snake, and it instantly attacked the arm. It sunk its teeth into the messenger's flesh and injected its venom.

The messenger screamed in pain and fear.

The scream threw the other messengers into a panic.

"Snake!"

"Where?"

"Where is it?"

Everyone was disoriented in the darkness. Another messenger stepped on the snake, and it hissed and bit again.

All three messengers bolted through the flap of the tent, yelling hysterically.

The warriors on night watch pulled burning logs from the campfire for torches.

"Where is it?" one of the warriors asked.

158

"In the tent!" the messenger replied feebly.

The warriors approached the tent, unfastened the pegs on one side, and lifted it. They looked inside and cautiously pulled back the clothes on the floor.

The black eyes of the snake flashed in the light of the torches.

The lead warrior pulled out his cutlass and cut off the snake's head in one fell swoop. The body twitched as its life ebbed away.

Necrosis started to set in for the first messenger. The second messenger shook from the effect of the venom and fear.

"Get me a small knife," the lead warrior demanded. He approached the men who had been bitten and held the arm of the first one. He observed the arm in the dim light and saw the puncture wounds from the snakebite. He made a thin cut to intersect both holes, sucked out the blood and venom, and spat it on the ground. "Do the same to him." He handed the dagger to another warrior, who sucked the venom out of the other messenger's leg.

The two warriors bandaged the wounds, but the poison was too far gone in the first servant's bloodstream.

The lead warrior said, "He may not make it. Give him water. We shall know by morning. Other than the watchers, I suggest you all go to sleep. We have a long day tomorrow."

The third messenger shook his head knowingly. "I told you there would be bad luck."

The warriors went to their tents, but the messengers opted to sleep out in the open. They were afraid of more snakes and would not risk being trapped in an enclosure again.

The sun's first rays exposed the corpse of the first messenger staring at the sky. The warriors closed his eyes and covered him with sand and bushes. There was no time for a proper burial.

"He is gone. There is nothing we can do," the lead warrior stated without emotion. He turned to the other snake-bitten messenger. "How do you feel?"

"I can manage," the messenger replied.

"Good. Let us continue our journey," the lead warrior said.

Everyone loaded their horses. They led the eleventh horse with no rider.

As they neared the walls of Odùduwà, the group paused.

The lead warrior instructed, "Let us wait until sundown. I understand that is when the warriors train. We shall have an advantage then if we must fight."

At sundown, they proceeded to the walls of Odùduwà. The formidable wall was three feet wide and twenty feet tall. Its hollow chambers housed the guards. King Àjosè's grandfather, Aláàfin Adésànyà, had built the walls. They had withstood many battles.

A sentry in the watchtower barked, "Who goes there?"

"We are emissaries from Hawani. We bring news for King Àjosè from King Guguwa."

Guards opened the gates and led the group to the courts.

King Àjosè and Àjàmú had just returned from the evening patrol and were discussing security matters.

A courtier instructed the men to wait in the outer courts and announced the visitors' arrival to the king.

"Ah, please have them enter," Àjosè said cordially.

The men were led to the inner courts. The lead messenger headed up the procession, flanked by the warriors.

"Your Highness, we bring a message from our king. After the experience here, he thought it necessary to send this message." He handed the note to the courtier, who handed it to the king.

King Àjosè read the note slowly. "I see. Guguwa declares war on Odùduwà." He looked at Àjàmú. "Perhaps we can remedy the situation. I thought we sent him away in peace, but I understand that more effort shall be required. Where are the escorts who accompanied the king to Hawani?"

"Your Highness, we are getting to that," the messenger said hesitantly.

The warriors glanced at each other and nodded. They looked around the court and assessed the situation. The warriors of Hawani were ready to defend themselves, just as Àmínù had advised.

CHAPTER 32

A True Warrior

The lead messenger handed the brown sack to the courtier, who handed it to the king.

Àjàmú walked up to Àjosè. "Your Highness, let me handle this." The general had always been in the habit of carrying his weapons with him wherever he went. He opened the bag, and the heads rolled out.

An unforgettable stench filled the court. The flesh had started to rot, and the skin had turned gray.

King Àjosè stood up. "What insolence! You dare to bring this to me! You dare to stand in my presence and deliver such a message?"

The warriors glanced knowingly at one another. The lead warrior repeated the general's instruction under his breath: "Defend yourselves if you must."

They nodded and posed in combat positions.

The lead warrior took out a dagger and threw it at King Àjosè, hoping to slay him right there.

Àjosè leaned sideways. The dagger barely missed him. "Àjàmú, throw me a cutlass!"

The general threw the king his cutlass and pulled out a small ax and a dagger from his waist.

The king's royal cloak flew off as he caught the cutlass in midair. "The gentleness of a lion should not be mistaken as cowardice!" he thundered.

Àjosè and Àjàmú moved toward the warriors briskly.

"Just like old times, my king," Àjàmú said with a slight smile. His ax was in one hand, and his dagger was in the other.

"Yes, just like old times." Àjosè swung at the closest warrior. Àjosè and Àjàmú pressed their backs against each other as they fought—the typical stance Odùduwà warriors employed when few men fought many adversaries.

The warriors from Hawani closed in on the king and the general. Two Hawani warriors attacked Àjosè with drawn cutlasses, and two others sprang toward Àjàmú.

"Legs," Àjàmú whispered.

Àjàmú and Àjosè turned in the opposite direction and faced each other's attackers. They crouched low as they spun.

Àjosè swung his cutlass, leaving deep gashes on the legs of one of the assailants.

Àjàmú slashed the legs of two attackers in one swing with his dagger and swung his ax with brute force that broke their legs simultaneously.

Àjosè thrust his cutlass into the stomach of another, leaving the first warrior on the floor.

Àjosè and Àjàmú stepped back. Their backs touched again as they surveyed the damage.

"Excellent move, my king," Àjàmú said.

"I have not forgotten our days as warriors. I was formidable," the king said with a grin.

Àjosè and Àjàmú were close friends and had both trained in the same regiment while growing up. The young prince had served as a commoner in the military, and Àjàmú—who came from a family of warriors—served alongside him. They loved to spar together. They both claimed superiority over one another, but the love they shared was immutable.

Amid the chaos, the courtier slipped out of the court to alert the guards.

"Kill them!" The lead Hawani warrior moved forward and brought his cutlass down toward Àjosè's head.

The king leaned backwards just in time and slightly eluded the tip of the blade.

The first warrior who attacked the king managed to rally. He lunged again.

Àjosè ducked and cut the warrior's thigh. He punched the lead Hawani warrior in the face as he rallied, causing him to lose balance momentarily. He thrust his cutlass into the first attacker's chest. As the warrior tumbled to the floor, his cutlass flew out of his hand.

Àjosè caught the cutlass midair in a swift motion upward and brought it down on the lead Hawani warrior, slicing from his rib cage down to his stomach. The lead warrior dropped to the floor.

Again, Àjàmú forcefully swung his ax at another warrior who had attacked him. The other two were writhing on the floor. The warrior had no means to shield the blow as Àjàmú's ax came down on his shoulders. Àjàmú retracted the blade, plunged his dagger into the warrior's chest, and swung at his head. The sound of his skull breaking echoed against the court walls. Àjàmú glanced back at King Àjosè.

The king picked up the cutlass of the dead warrior.

Another pair of warriors attacked. Àjosè blocked the attack with both cutlasses and took a step forward, lunging between them. He crossed his hands and made a wide arc as he swung, cutting off their heads. He looked down as the heads hit the floor. Àjàmú smiled. *This man is still a true warrior.*

Commotion erupted as several Odùduwà warriors rushed into the inner courts, filled with rage. They had received the courtier's message that the king was under attack.

Àjosè kicked the last Hawani warrior toward the Odùduwà warriors. They plunged several daggers into his torso and cut off his head before he could hit the floor. Àjàmú stepped back as the warriors finished off the two aggressors with broken legs.

"Leave the messengers," King Àjosè instructed. "We shall send them back with the heads of their warriors."

All eight heads were placed into the same brown sacks that had carried the slain Odùduwà servants. King Àjosè handed the freshly bloodied sacks to the messengers. Justice had been swift.

"You are a true warrior, my king," Àjàmú marveled.

"We had no choice. We shall give Guguwa what he wants," stated Àjosè.

"I stand by you, my king," Àjàmú replied.

"I never intended it to come to this," the king remarked woefully.

Àjàmú walked out of the courts to oversee the dispatch of the messengers back to Hawani. It would give him something to do other than grieve his son's death.

The queen walked into the king's bedroom in the middle of the night. Adélolá needed to be with Àjosè. The thought of almost losing him due to his ailment, plus the near assassination that evening, filled her with insecurity. She could not bear the thought of anything happening to her husband. He was not in his room. She walked into the court and found the king sitting on his throne. "What is wrong, my king? Why are you not in bed?"

"I was incapacitated for a few days and awoke to this! Now we are at war with Hawani. In the past, the kingdoms of the north and south were always at war. Many lives and riches were lost. We have struggled for years to keep the peace, but now history is repeating itself on our soil, during my reign!"

Adélolá felt stricken with guilt. "My lord, what was I supposed to do? If you were in my situation, what would you have done? I thought the man was responsible for your ailment. I could not let him go until things were clarified."

Àjosè stared at her and shook his head.

"We have no choice now. Maybe it is for the best. Guguwa has crossed many lines in the past. This may be a good time to make an example of him." King Àjosè got up and walked to his chambers.

Adélolá followed him.

"I would like to be alone for now. Have a good night, Adélolá." He turned and walked to his chambers.

The queen stared at his figure as he disappeared into his room. She choked back tears as she returned to her own bed.

CHAPTER 33

Prelude to the Inferno

Àjàmú dispatched the messengers to Hawani. "Tell your king we are ready for war. We shall meet him on the battlefield two fortnights from today."

The messengers contemplated the events as they rode back.

"I knew things were going to go awry. You cannot see a vulture circle you three times, land, and stare at you—and then ignore it!"

The second messenger shrugged. "We delivered the message, and we are alive to deliver the reply. We have successfully carried out our duties."

They approached the burial spot of the messenger who had been bitten by the snake. His body was only partially covered in sand and bushes. Wild animals and vultures had discovered it and were feasting on the corpse. They both looked away; it could have been them. After their encounter at the Odùduwà kingdom, they were too rattled to stop and rest. They rode all day and all night.

Upon arrival at Hawani, the messengers relayed what had transpired in Odùduwà.

"I told you they wanted war!" King Guguwa bellowed. "We shall give it to them. Sound the drums!"

King Guguwa commanded his generals to prepare for war.

Àmínù the Madawaki spearheaded the preparation. The warriors practiced battle formations, and workmen began to craft weaponry. Hawani was known for its arrows. They had skilled archers and powerful bows. The aerodynamic design of the arrows allowed them to travel great distances, serving as the first line of attack against enemies.

In previous battles, Hawani had been known to perform sudden retreats. Archers would continue the offense until the cavalry had regrouped and resumed the carnage. Few enemies could stand their deadly strategy.

"I still do not believe we should engage in this war," Garzo confided to Dambo and Tanko.

"What was done to the king is inexcusable," Dambo said haughtily.

"I am in agreement with you, Elder Dambo," Garzo replied, "but instead of an explicit confrontation, we could have used the situation as leverage to negotiate for concessions from Odúduwà—maybe even weaken them and attack them covertly. An explicit confrontation shall not yield the results we desire."

"Are you saying that we are not strong enough to dominate Odúduwà?" Dambo challenged.

"I doubt it. They are the dominant kingdom in the region for a reason. They are not to be trifled with. If it had been easy to overpower Odúduwà, our king would have done so long ago. Would you not agree?"

Tanko spoke up. "What do you suggest we do, then, Elder Garzo?"

"I shall attempt to impress upon the king that this is not the time for pride. We need allies. In the interim, I suggest you all hide your valuables. Send some to relatives and have a contingency plan in case our plans do not work out in our favor."

Queen Adélolá walked into the inner courts.

King Àjosè was sitting with Fádèyí, Àjàmú, Kúyè, and some elders. "I am not going to beg Guguwa. We sent him away honorably. We apologized and assigned him escorts to establish the lines of diplomacy.

We hoped to do more to remedy the situation, but look at what he did in return." The king's white *agbádá* swept the floor as he shifted on his throne. He adjusted the right and left sides and folded the bottom part between his legs. "I do not care for war, but if it is brought to our doorstep, we shall not shy away from it. We are the premier kingdom in this region, and that shall not change under my rule. I shall not allow others to think they can get away with such actions."

Àjàmú nodded. "Killing our servants and sending warriors to assassinate the king is unforgivable."

"In the palace!" one of the elders exclaimed.

"It is treacherous," Kúyè added. "He has given no room for peace!"

Those who passed the royal chambers overheard the raised voices and scurried along. This was serious business.

"Your Highness, Guguwa has always challenged you. You know how he feels about Odùduwà's leadership in these environs. It is time we put an end to his insolence." Àjàmú stood and wrung his hands behind his back. His muscular arms tensed as he spoke. The bands embedded with cowries stretched as he flexed his biceps and deltoids. He was ready for war. Anyone and everyone who could would pay for the death of Àjàní.

The queen finally spoke up. "Your Majesty, can we pressure Hawani to not drag us into war? Perhaps we can send another message to King Guguwa."

"Lolá, we shall talk at a later time," King Àjosè answered shortly. "I am busy with my advisers!"

The court went silent.

The queen knelt and quietly left the court.

"Your Highness, may I speak with you alone?" Fádèyí's tone of voice indicated a sober conversation.

Àjosè dismissed Kúyè, Àjàmú, and the elders. The sound of shuffling feet faded into the shadows of the corridors.

The king faced Fádèyí squarely. "You have my attention, my lord." Even though Àjosè was king, he had a deep respect for the chief priest. He was an elder according to Odùduwà tradition, and he had been like a second father to him. He had taught and advised him ever since the untimely death of his natural father.

Fádèyí began, "The queen did not intend this consequence—although she is not without fault. There is enough blame to go around. Do not be angry with her. It shall not help the situation. Sometimes, in the design of destiny, we play roles we have no intention of playing. We do not have as much control over life as we like to think." Fádèyí put his hand on Àjosè's shoulder. "You are like a son to me, so I speak to you as I would my son."

"And you stand in the place of a father to me," the king replied pensively.

"This shall be a difficult battle. Do not think you shall easily annihilate Hawani and restore peace and order. The whispers of the oracles say this shall profoundly change Odúduwà. I am not sure how, but you must make all preparations. King Guguwa shall be a formidable foe."

"What do you suggest I do, Bàbá?" Àjosè asked.

"You must send for allies. I shall speak with Àjàmú, and we shall draw up battle strategies."

Àjosè approved. "I shall heed your advice, Bàbá. We shall dispatch messages immediately."

At daybreak, Odúduwà dispatched messengers to the Ashanti and Dahomey kingdoms. Walls around the kingdom were fortified, and trenches were dug. There was excitement in the air as everyone prepared. Odúduwà intended to take the fight to the enemy, but if the battle were brought to Odúduwà, the kingdom would be prepared. It would certainly lead to their enemies' demise.

Àjàmú and Sòbògun were training the warriors in the field, sharpening their skills for battle.

Sòbògun was a short and stocky man with a big belly, but those who mistook his form for lack of capacity got a rude awakening. "Move to the left! If someone charges at you like he did, you move to the left!" Sòbògun roared at one of the newer warriors.

"What about oil?" Àjàmú asked.

Sòbògun replied, "We have cauldrons of oil at all the towers, and we have saddled fifty horses with bags of oil." He was solely responsible for the infantry. He had fought many wars; the battle scars on his face and body proved it. He was respected by the warriors.

The newer warriors were barely awake. They had risen before sunrise, but if they showed any drowsiness, they were struck by the older warriors. There was no tolerance for unpreparedness or weakness. Àjàmú believed the army was as weak as its weakest warrior. Everyone was pushed to their breaking point, allowed to recover, and made to start again.

"Àjàmú!" Fádèyí called across the training ground.

Àjàmú sighed and walked up to Fádèyí. He had no time for talking this early in the morning. "My lord?"

"I wish to give you a word of advice. I understand you want to avenge the death of your son. I see you are pushing the warriors hard. This may be good or bad, but before you go to war, I suggest you put your house in order."

Àjàmú furrowed his brow. "Is that what you saw in the ifá oracle?"

"No, I did not see anything, General. It is not a prophecy. I am simply giving you fatherly advice."

The air was laden with moisture, and the morning sun was starting to show its strength. On the other side of the sky, rain clouds were forming.

Àjàmú was eager to continue with preparations. If he was not happy with their progress by the time the rain started, they would continue in the rain. "Thank you, Bàbá Fádèyí. If you shall excuse me." He bowed slightly. *If this is where I meet death, I shall take ten thousand enemies along with me,* the general thought as he walked back to meet the warriors.

Lightning flashed across the eastern sky.

Wooden cutlasses clashed, and sticks representing spears collided. The rain came down in torrents.

"Continue!" Àjàmú yelled to Sòbògun.

"My lord." Sòbògun bowed. He turned to the drenched warriors. "Continue training!"

CHAPTER 34

Love and War

The birds of Odùduwà chirped harmoniously in the early morning.

Sinmi was barely awake, listening to the familiar sounds in the background. The music of nature was calming, but one particular chirp had a higher pitch. Sinmi sat up quickly. *It is Labí! They must be training.* She quietly strolled out through the back of the house.

Labí peered through the bushes. He did not want to risk being seen by Sinmi's parents: they would not be enthused to see him luring their daughter into the bushes.

Ever since Labí had met Sinmi at the festival—the night Dépò had harassed her—he had fallen for her. And she had fallen for him. Sinmi had been shaken by Dépò's abrasiveness, thus Labí began to accompany her home. Dépò was not happy to lose to Labí, but the animosity between them had given way to a strong friendship. Suffering and facing death together had forged a bond that erased any jealousy toward the other.

Odùduwà was famous for its brooms. Long canes were whittled into thin strands of various thicknesses: the thinner-stranded brooms to collect and move mass as they swept, and the thicker-stranded brooms to pick up litter.

Sinmi had to create an alibi. She picked up a long broom and walked toward the chirping bird. When Labí appeared laughing, she ran into his arms. "What are you doing here so early?"

"You know we have our race every week," Labí answered mischievously.

"And why have you left the race? You shall get yourself in trouble," Sinmi warned.

"Don't worry, I was ahead of most of them. I know the terrain. Besides, we have some new warriors who lag behind."

"You don't want to win the race? You always like to win." Sinmi's eyes danced as she gazed into Labí's.

"You know the situation," he said quietly. He let go of her and took a step back. "Ever since Àjàní's passing, I do not feel the need to compete anymore. I mean, things are just different. Who am I going to do all that with now? Dépò?"

"Well, you two have become friends since your mission together," Sinmi said. "Though I'm not thrilled you two are friends."

"He isn't a bad person, really, if you get to know him," Labí replied.

"If I got to know him?" Sinmi asked playfully. "Very well then, I shall get to know him."

"Not *know* him in that sense," Labí said quickly. "There is a brotherhood among the warriors, especially the elites like us."

"Hmm." Sinmi smiled.

Labí returned the smile. "Some of them are a little insane, but those are the ones you want to go to war with."

Sinmi crossed her arms. "Well, when you come here, leave that brotherhood behind. I don't want to deal with that type of insanity."

"Yes, Mà." Labí smiled, pulled Sinmi toward him, and slapped her derrière.

Sinmi pushed him away. "You want to get me in trouble? My father shall kill you!"

Labí laughed.

Sinmi's father had threatened to kill Labí before; he too had once been a warrior. One early morning in the past, Labí had come looking for Sinmi. When he noticed a man in the backyard with his daughter, he charged out of the house with a cutlass and chased Labí up a tree.

Sinmi ran to get her mother.

"My dear, calm down," Sinmi's mother told her husband.

"I shall kill him!" Sinmi's father hollered. He brandished his cutlass and pointed it toward Labí in the tree. "And you!" He turned to Sinmi and tried to hit her.

Sinmi's mother grabbed his hand. "She is not a child anymore. You cannot do that. Besides, don't you want her to get married? Are you going to marry her yourself?"

"If she comes home pregnant before getting married, I shall disown both of you," Sinmi's father growled.

"My lord, I shall take responsibility." She knelt in front of him and signaled to Sinmi to do the same.

Sinmi stood back. She did not want to be whipped.

"Come!" her mother insisted.

Sinmi knelt beside her mother.

Sinmi's father was disarmed by their demonstration of respect. He loved them too much.

"Young man, come down from the tree," Sinmi's mother said. "Come here."

Labí climbed down sheepishly.

He lay prostrate beside the kneeling women and clasped the ankles of Sinmi's father. "Bàbá, please forgive me."

Sinmi's parents burst out laughing.

"Boy, don't make an old man like me to fall," Sinmi's father quipped. "What is your name?"

"Labí is my name, Your Highness ... I mean, my lord." Labí looked up but dared not meet his gaze directly.

"He is a jester," Sinmi's father said to his wife. "Your daughter brought home a jester!"

Sinmi's mother ignored the comment. "Are you the same Labí who won the hunting competition with Àjàní?"

"Yes, Mà," Labí replied.

Sinmi's mother turned to her husband. "My lord, this boy is a great warrior. These are the men who make Odùduwà great."

Thank the gods for good fame, Labí thought.

"He is friends with Àjàmú's son, Àjàní," Sinmi's mother said.

The father's countenance softened a bit. Àjàmú was respected in the land, and anyone connected to him would be given the benefit of the doubt. He had mourned Àjàní's death along with all of Odùduwà. "Very well, get up."

Labí stood. He was tall and handsome, and he had an unruly beard and mustache. It was hard not to like the man.

"Take care of my daughter," he said as he returned to the hut. His cutlass swung back and forth around his waist as he moved.

"Sinmi, be careful next time. You know how your father is," Sinmi's mother warned.

"Màmá, I've mentioned him to you before. You know how Bàbá is. That's why I didn't tell him. That's why we sneak around like this. I am not a child anymore, you know."

"You did not say all that in front of your father. You have a mouth to talk. Next time, you shall defend yourself." Sinmi's mother rolled her eyes. "Anyway, Labí, welcome. Please let us know when you come next so we can prepare for you. Come through the front door next time and greet Bàbá if he is home. Do not sneak around the back. Greet your mother when you get home. I shall watch for her when I go to the market." Sinmi's mother gave her daughter a stern look and went to join her husband in the hut.

"You see?" Sinmi glared at Labí.

"I am not afraid. There is no fear where there is love," Labí boasted.

"Hmmm, there is no fear, eh? You, the coward who ran to climb the tree!" Sinmi laughed.

"*Èmi,* Jagunlabì the brave one." Labí smiled and hit his chest.

"*Ódáa ná,*" (Very well then) Sinmi replied with a smile.

"I shall see you tomorrow." Labí ran off.

Sinmi chuckled. "This man shall get me in trouble."

Sinmi would visit Labí when he trained. Whenever she showed up, Labí would put in extra effort. Anyone training with Labí knew the trend. He did not want Sinmi to see him as weak. Whenever others knew she was around, they made catcalls, which angered both Labí and the commanders.

When Sinmi was ill, Labí refused to go to training. He knew he would be punished, but he stayed by her side until she was well. Labí paid the price when he returned to the training camp after a six-day hiatus. Sóbógun would make Labí walk miles with a huge log tied to his shoulders.

When the warriors went on a mission, Sinmi refused to eat until they came back. Her mother begged her to eat to no avail. Few were as happy as Sinmi to hear news of the warriors' return. She too had mourned the death of Àjàní. She sought to alleviate the sadness that overcame Labí, but she did not know how to comfort him. He cried for days and confined himself to his home. She finally convinced him to come out of mourning when she threatened to harm herself if he remained in his depressed state.

The next morning came. True to his word, Labí returned before sunrise.

Sinmi heard the special bird calling. She hurried out the back door, grabbing a broom on the way.

The pair held each other's hands, talking and laughing until the sun peeked over the horizon.

"You should go, Labí. People are up, and someone may see you. Otherwise, come through the front door and ask to see me. I'm not sure what excuse you shall give my parents this time. Besides, you must finish your race before you get in trouble again."

The family cat snuck up to Sinmi and rubbed itself on her legs, letting its tail linger as it sniffed Labí.

Labí squatted and stroked the brown and white cat. It purred and stared at him with its big hazel eyes.

"I know, but I must talk with you about something, Sinmi," Labí said in a serious tone. "I've been thinking about us."

"I've been thinking about us too, my love."

"Have you heard the news?" Labí asked.

"What news?" Sinmi probed.

"The king of Hawani has declared war on Odùduwà." Labí took a deep breath. "This shall delay things with us. I thought we could make things happen sooner than later."

"Did the king not apologize and send him off with gifts?" Sinmi shook her head. "I don't want you to go to war. I cannot afford to lose you, Labí."

"I know, my love, but I have to go. This is the way of warriors," Labí stated matter-of-factly.

Sinmi knelt and looked up at him. "Labí, please promise me you shall come back alive."

"I promise." Labí gazed affectionately at Sinmi and took another deep breath. *No time like the present.* "Sinmi, will you marry me?"

Sinmi's hand flew to her mouth.

"Sinmi, will you be my wife?"

"Yes, yes, I will, my love! I love you so—"

"Sinmi!" Sinmi's mother called out.

Labí kissed her tenderly. "We shall get married after the war. As soon as I return, I shall come for you, my darling." He disappeared into the forest and rejoined the race.

"What are you doing over there?" Sinmi's mother asked.

"I was sweeping the compound, Mà," Sinmi lied.

Sinmi's mother eyed her daughter suspiciously. "Sinmi, you are holding the wrong broom."

CHAPTER 35

Negotiations

It was late in the evening when the delegation from Odùduwà arrived in Dahomey. They were led into the courts, where King Drogba was seated with his advisers. Emissaries from Hawani had already arrived and were making their petition.

"Stand over there." The courtier led the group from Odùduwà over to the group from Hawani. There was a brief silence as they gathered.

The lead emissary from Hawani said, "As I was saying, Your Highness, our king was thrown into their dungeon and disgraced. Àjosè was revived—"

"You shall address him as *King* Àjosè," one of the messengers from Odùduwà snipped.

"He is not my king." The speaker spat on the floor. The bile landed beside the foot of the emissary from Odùduwà.

A fight broke out between the two groups. Fists flew, and clothes were torn.

"Stop, stop!" Ológun demanded.

Mino warriors pried the two groups apart.

King Drogba said, "The two kingdoms shall give their petitions separately. Take the messengers from Odùduwà outside. They shall present their case after the messengers from Hawani."

"Swine," hissed an emissary from Odùduwà on the way out.

"Fools!" retorted one from Hawani.

The lead messenger from Hawani resumed his speech. "And that was how we came by this war, Your Highness. Odùduwà must be taught a lesson. We understand the oppression that Odùduwà has imposed on you, as it has on us. We seek your help in putting Odùduwà in its place. We want to know if Dahomey shall join us in this holy war."

King Drogba adjusted his garments. "We have heard you. Now we shall hear from Odùduwà. We shall inform you of our position in the morning." He raised his hand to signal the end of the consultation.

The Odùduwà delegation entered to present their case. "We pleaded with King Guguwa. We sent him home with gifts and escorts."

"You thought gifts would assuage the situation?" King Drogba asked with a smirk.

"No, Your Highness. These were gestures to allow for continued rectification of the wrong."

Drogba shook his head and turned to his queen. "You see what I've been telling you about Odùduwà? But when I speak, you admonish me." He turned back to the speaker. "Continue."

"Upon arrival in Hawani, our escorts were beheaded."

Gasps rose from those present. This was an abhorrent act—even in Dahomey.

Princess Fazilah stood. Gbàjà gestured for the princess to sit down. This was not the time to speak.

"They returned the heads of our escorts to us through a cohort of warriors and messengers. They declared war, but their real intent was to assassinate King Àjosè. They met him and his general in the inner court and attacked him. He and his general fought the warriors. If not for the bravery of our king and our general, he would have been killed. We beheaded the warriors and sent their heads back to Hawani with the messengers. We had no choice but to accept the challenge for war."

Once the representatives from Odùduwà had finished, King Drogba dismissed them. Servants led them to their accommodations.

King Drogba, Gbàjà, Bira, and some other advisers consulted all night. Queen Témbè and Princess Fazilah were also present to observe the deliberations.

"What say you, Gbàjà?" King Drogba asked.

They had to answer in the morning. Any decision would be a turning point for Dahomey. If they stayed neutral, Odùduwà might exact revenge. The absence of King Drogba in regional ceremonies, especially with an invitation, had already set the stage for Dahomey to be admonished by Odùduwà.

Should Dahomey stand with Hawani, defeat Odùduwà, and hope to evade immense loss during the war? Dahomey could gain the right to become independent, but it also risked becoming a vassal of Hawani. King Guguwa could not be entirely trusted, but allying with Odùduwà against Hawani would mean continued subservience to Odùduwà, which Dahomey had grown tired of. The taxation was heavy, and Odùduwà's control of Dahomey's trade routes had become contentious.

Gbàjà's steady voice conveyed wisdom. "Your Highness, I say we stay neutral, but prepare for battle without their knowledge. We shall watch closely as the war proceeds. At a later point, we shall decide whether to join this war. This way, we shall be in a better position to determine what is in our best interests."

"Bira, what say you?" the king asked.

"The oracle has spoken well, Your Highness. We must stay neutral for now."

"You have spoken well, Gbàjà," Queen Témbè added. "In the meantime, I shall send word to my people of these developments."

"I too agree with the oracle," Princess Fazilah added.

Early the next morning, the delegations from Odùduwà and Hawani prepared to receive the king's answer.

A courtier arrived at the chambers of the Odùduwà group. "The king shall see you now."

King Drogba sat on his throne, appearing uninterested.

Elder Bira handed a letter to the group. "This is a letter to your king. Dahomey shall not partake in the war. The letter clarifies the reason."

The lead messenger approached the throne but was blocked by two guards. "O King, we beseech you—"

Bira said, "The king's word is final. Dahomey shall not be involved in the war. You may now leave."

The delegation from Hawani entered the courts, and the group from Odùduwà snarled at them as they exited. The emissaries from Hawani were also handed a letter to deliver to their king.

"We shall not be a part of the war. The letter shall give your king clarity."

The group from Hawani was dismissed. Dahomey's position was sealed.

Lúlù watched from afar as both groups rode off. *There will be war in Odùduwà.* Regardless of the turn of events, she still had a soft spot for Odùduwà. It was her home.

Her child crawled up to her and tugged at her legs.

Lúlù picked up her son.

The baby watched the horses kicking up billows of dust as they galloped toward their respective kingdoms. His eyes glowed a soft blue as he looked back at his mother.

Lúlù gazed tenderly into her baby's eyes. "I wonder what you see, little one. I wonder what you see."

CHAPTER 36

The Golden Stool I

The Ashanti kingdom would soon host its annual regional market gathering in Kumasi. As was customary, the Odùduwà kingdom sent a group of vendors that included members from kingdoms under their control. They traveled together for safety and to help each other carry their goods. Combining human and material resources also put the traders in a better position to barter for goods that fueled commercial activities back home. Wealthy members of society would hire representatives to carry their goods or conduct business on their behalf.

Each regional market across the land of Alkebulan specialized in certain goods and services. The gathering in Kumasi focused on the exchange of gold and other precious metals for ironwork and tools. It was also possible to buy clothes, salt, and slaves, but those were more common in the Songhai Empire in the north. The Songhai market was an even bigger gathering that drew people from other parts of the world.

It was common to share news and knowledge at the gatherings. Traders often regaled themselves with stories of their kingdoms and foreign lands. Stories were often exaggerated, but one could sift through the hyperbole and gain a fairly accurate picture of current events.

King Àjosè called on Iyìolá, the chief in charge of trade, to ask about the delegation to Kumasi.

Iyìolá was known for his strong business acumen. He had helped steer the kingdom through many crises. He was flamboyant. It was rare to see him without his flowing agbádá and a servant carrying his goods. He was always ready to make a trade.

"Iyìolá, where do we stand with preparations for the Kumasi market?" King Àjosè asked.

"Your Highness." Iyìolá's agbádá swept the ground as he prostrated himself before the king.

"Please rise, Iyìolá. Where do we stand with preparations for the market day?" the king asked.

Iyìolá was a man who took pride in his sense of fashion. He adjusted his agbádá as he stated, "We have produced many implements of war. We have more than one thousand knives, spears, and cutlasses. We have shields and armor, and several blacksmiths and ironworkers have produced intricate arts and crafts. I know these wares shall command a high value at the market. We are behind, however, in the production of armor for the horses. The new design is difficult for the novice blacksmiths. Onírin died last year, and the son is not as proficient as the father." He adjusted his agbádá again. "Even if we do not produce as much armor as we hope, the few we have shall spark the interest of the Ashanti, Fulani, and other kingdoms in attendance. Perhaps we can arrange to make deliveries before the next market cycle."

Iyìolá's detailed report impressed King Àjosè. He was reliable and astute. He was an Ìjèbú man, and if the Ìjèbús were known for one thing, it was their shrewdness when it came to business.

"Which kingdoms have confirmed they shall send market representatives with our delegation?" King Àjosè asked.

"Every surrounding kingdom has confirmed representatives except for Dahomey," Iyìolá replied.

"Let us wait and see what they do," the king mused. "As a vassal state, I expect them to join our convoy."

In the past, Odùduwà had fought and won many wars with Dahomey, which had brought the kingdom under Odùduwà's control, but Dahomey still enjoyed a large degree of autonomy. Àjosè did not relish the thought of a confrontation with Dahomey—or any kingdom. Nonetheless, he would not allow any kingdom to defy Odùduwà. It would set a negative precedent, which would likely precede other challenges to their power and culminate in a large-scale revolt or assault.

Àjosè's father, King Adégòkè, had been a fierce warrior. He had been renowned for his strength and authority in the region. He had been the *ààre ònà kakañfò*, (the supreme military commander) of Odùduwà, before he became king. He had taught Àjosè the ways of the Yorùbá warriors: honor and forthrightness. Kings of the subjected kingdoms frequently challenged King Àjosè's authority, sensing he was not as prone to war as his father. As King Àjosè pondered recent events in the kingdom, he remembered his father's words: "To keep the peace, one must project power."

Kumasi bustled with excitement as the regional market drew closer. Goldsmiths worked day and night. The primary commodity that merchants sought in the Kumasi market was the gold of the Ashanti kingdom. People came from far and wide to barter with the Ashanti people and other merchants. When the traders arrived, other businesses would thrive. The gathering lasted three days, and at that time, the demand for food in the city would go up. People would need accommodations and cleaning services. There would be entertainment and festivities every night.

King Kofi II called for Anokye, his trusted chief priest and adviser. "Has the golden stool been thoroughly cleaned?"

"Yes, Your Highness," Anokye responded.

The golden stool was the divine throne of the kings and a symbol of power and royalty for the Ashanti people. It was heavy—made of pure gold—and required two strong men to carry it. The golden stool was never to touch the ground, and no one was allowed to sit on it, including the king.

The stool was kept in a secret place. It was believed that the spirits of dead kings stopped to rest on the stool as they passed through the kingdom. Many wars had been fought over the stool. King Kofi II had established a ritual under his rule to show the stool to only a few important Ashantis and to foreigners on the last day of the Kumasi market. The stool reminded the Ashantis that King Kofi II was still in possession of the stool and controlled its powers. It also propagated his fame and legend to foreign lands.

"Your Highness, shall the stool be exhibited once again this year?" Anokye asked.

"You have asked me this question in times past, Anokye. My answer has not changed," the king responded irritably.

"If I may be allowed to speak as I did with your father," Anokye pressed. "I know that exhibiting the stool propagates your power, but it also exposes the stool to theft and may lead to conflict."

"This is precisely why I show it, Anokye. I want to remind my enemies—at home and abroad—of my power. When they behold the stool, they shall remember my power, and they shall dare not incite conflict." The king respected Anokye and was close to him. Anokye's advice had saved him from many troubles. However, sometimes he could not help but think that Anokye's ways were ancient. He lacked the strategy and foresight of the newer world. Empires were being built. Discoveries were being made. Not all conflicts were won with hand-to-hand battle and petty squabbles. Soft power and strategic alliances were taking the place of sporadic conflicts. He may have to advise Anokye of this at some point, but he would reserve it for another time.

The king's vibrant red, green, and yellow wrapper contrasted beautifully against his black skin, gold armbands, and gold headband. Ashanti was surely the land of gold. "Please inform the treasurer that I request his presence. I want to know how much gold we possess and what our focus shall be for purchases this year. They must be in line with the strategy of our kingdom. Thank you, Anokye."

"Your Highness," Anokye said, stroking his white beard as he walked away. He remembered the saying of an elderly foreign trader from the east: "A young man's glory is in his strength, but the gray hairs of experience are the splendor of an old man."

King Kofi II sat back in his chair and stared into the distance. *This year, I will further establish my kingdom. I have a powerful army and money to buy weapons.*

The Odùduwàs were renowned for their ironwork. King Kofi II would have his general, Odom, buy their best armor before the first day of the market. *It may be wise to subdue the Baoule people and take control of the ivory trade.*

The market gathering would commence the following day. Men from all over Akebu land started to arrive in Kumasi. Excitement filled the air as merchants set up their stalls to display their wares. People thronged the market paths. Many people attended just to peruse the vast array of goods on display. The first day was usually a day of exhibition. Transactions normally took place on the second day. Whatever was left, which was normally not the best, was sold on the third day.

Merchants from other regions, including the Songhai Empire, were known for the great knowledge they possessed. They were advanced in medicine, and they normally sent a contingent to see local patients and perform operations. People waited for the arrival of the Songhai doctors to treat ailments that the local doctors could not address. A woman was going blind, but the doctors from Songhai had performed a cataract operation and restored her vision, which was unprecedented at the time. The doctors were particular to avoid being praised. They practiced the religion of Islam, which promoted a high level of propriety. They were greatly respected by the people.

The guild from Odùduwà and the subsidiary kingdoms arrived, but the Dahomey people were conspicuously absent.

King Kofi sent Odom to greet the group and help them locate a corner lot with significant traffic. He also provided help to set up their wares.

Odom said, "The king sends his warmest regards. He insists that whatever you need to make your journey a success, you should communicate to me." He was a burly man who exuded strength, power, and authority. A wrapper covered the lower half of his muscular body, and four chains made of bright red beads—two on each shoulder—crossed his torso. "The king wishes to know the goods you seek before they are made available to other merchants. You shall be compensated for your accommodation."

Iyìolá smiled. *So, this is what the preferential treatment is about. Well, it shall be mutually beneficial. I shall acquire as much gold as possible from the Ashanti king.*

CHAPTER 37

The Golden Stool II

Dusk fell upon Kumasi. Visitors chattered excitedly about the evening's entertainment. Local and foreign groups staged delightful plays, but the story of the golden stool was the most anticipated performance. Every year, the Ashanti people reenacted the legend of the golden stool on the last night of the gathering. Osei Kofi Tutu I, the current king's father, had founded the Ashanti Empire in collaboration with the chief priest. A coalition of Asante states had formed a united front to challenge the prevailing power at the time, the Denkyira.

The Asante people had defeated Denkyira and made it a tributary to the Ashanti kingdom. The play narrated how the priest invoked the golden stool from heaven and brought it down to the lap of King Osei Tutu I. Although no one had witnessed the event, the stool was revered by all. King Osei Tutu II possessed and controlled it, which gave him spiritual authority and deference from the people. The play always took place at night to display the golden stool in all its glory.

The first night ended with the usual excitement, and prospective transactions were determined. The king was satisfied since he had already secured the best arms and tools from the Odùduwà people.

Iyìolá was equally pleased. *With the amount of gold I shall receive from trading directly with the king, it shall be easy to further our economic interests. My group can enjoy the rest of their stay in Kumasi.* On the second day, Iyìolá combed the market for women selling kenke and banku with tilapia. He enjoyed the Ashanti food. He came across a crowd that had formed around a few men and pushed his way to the front.

The men in the middle had skin that was cherry-red from exposure to the sun. They were serving a colored fluid from a wooden drum. Shortly after the recipients drank the fluid, they started to laugh and dance hysterically. They seemed to be inebriated—as if they had drank too much palm wine—but this one had a much quicker and stronger effect.

"Who are these people?" Iyìolá asked a man in the crowd.

"They are Portuguese, from a faraway land. They have visited the coast for many years and dealt with the Denkyira. Now that the Ashantis control the coast, our king has improved relations with them. More of them now visit Ashanti land. You have never heard of them?"

"I have, but I have never met a Portuguese man myself," Iyìolá replied.

"You should try the drink. You shall never forget it."

Iyìolá stepped forward, paid the fee, and demanded a cup. As he drank it, he felt a strong burning sensation in his throat. He gagged but managed to push it down. After all, he had paid for it. He felt a warm sensation as it made its way to his stomach.

A Portuguese man suggested he take a seat.

"I feel fine," Iyìolá said.

"I would advise you sit for a moment," the man said in the Twi language.

Iyìolá obliged, but after a few minutes, he decided to get up. He stood abruptly and staggered as a wave of dizziness overcame him. After a short period, it cleared. He then started to feel happy and inclined to dance to the music. He had not danced like this in years. He had a few more cups and started to dance furiously. A part of him wondered about the lack of inhibition, but by that time, he was too drunk to care. The last thing he remembered was admiring the beautiful sunset. He reached out to touch the sun and fell backward.

The stranger ran over, grabbed him before he hit the ground, and dragged him to a shaded tree.

On the third and final day, merchants frantically tried to dispose of their wares with last-minute deals. Some were happy with the deals they had struck, but there were obvious losers. One could pick them out by their sullen looks.

When evening came, visitors and citizens alike gathered in the palace court. The court had six pillars, each adorned with elaborate patterns of gold and deep red paint. The king's throne boasted two lions made of solid gold on either side. The queen's throne was positioned to the left of the king's throne. High chiefs formed a semicircle to the left and right of the king. The queen and the warriors stood behind them.

King Kofi II called on Anokye to coordinate the exhibition of the stool.

Ten warriors appeared at the court entrance. They split into two rows of five with the stool between them.

The local populace and foreigners made way as the warriors marched through the crowd with the golden stool on a crate. An elegant white linen covered the stool, hiding it from view until the grand exhibition.

King Kofi II had been waiting for this moment. This display of authority was an excellent precursor to the expansionary quest he was about to undertake.

The crate was placed on a platform in front of the throne. The king rose. "Welcome, my chiefs, honorable guests, foreign envoys, merchants, and the great people of the Ashanti kingdom. I thank you for gracing the courts with your presence. I thank you for partaking of this gathering and for considering Kumasi your regional market center. The kingdom shall continue to host you and ensure your time here is comfortable. Thank you all for coming."

The crowd applauded.

Iyìolá still had a headache from the day before. He could not remember what had happened. He had awoken in the guest quarters, but he still did not know how he had arrived there.

King Kofi II took one last sweep of the crowd before sitting down. His eyes caught Iyìolá's.

Iyìolá bowed discreetly to the king in spite of his headache.

The king made a slight gesture in his direction to acknowledge the arms deal they had brokered three days prior.

Food and drinks were served to everyone. It was stately and conservative, but the real celebration would begin after the unveiling of the stool.

After dinner, Anokye stood up.

The drummers started to pound the royal drums.

"Thank you all for attending this royal banquet. The greatness of our king and our kingdom cannot be underestimated. We have shown far and wide that we are a people to be reckoned with. We are about to show you the symbol of Ashanti power. The golden stool came from above. The gods have seen it fit to bless us and to redeem the Ashanti people from all their years of suffering. Under the command of His Royal Highness, King Kofi II—and in response to the voice of the people—I give you the golden stool." He raised his arm high and dropped it.

Two warriors pulled the white silk cloth off the golden stool.

The twenty-four torches in the darkened court illuminated the golden stool. The crowd hushed in awe of the magnificent object.

The Portuguese men stared at the golden stool and whispered to one another.

Anokye motioned to the musicians, and they started to play festive music. Maids flooded the court with trays of strong drinks. The drinking and celebrating lasted well into the night. Around midnight, the stool was covered and taken to the inner courts.

King Kofi II felt drunk with glee. *The expansion of my kingdom shall commence soon. I shall make my father proud and prove the naysayers wrong. Some say I cannot last on the throne as my father did. Some say I am not as great as my father. Some say I lack intellect and foresight. They shall soon know how capable I am.* He fell asleep with his two royal concubines on either side of his bed.

"Akoko, be quiet," Anokye yelled to a rooster.

The gold and black rooster—a gift to the queen from a past envoy from Dahomey—seemed to particularly enjoy the tree near his bedroom window. The rooster was said to have special abilities and served as a watchman, but Anokye did not buy it. He would have killed it if the queen did not have such a fondness for it. This morning, it would not stop crowing and beating its wings frantically.

"This is madness. Stupid rooster." Anokye stood up, tied his wrapper, and looked out his window. "Shut up. It is still dark. Why are you up so early?"

The rooster flew down from the branch and beat its wings in Anokye's face.

"Enough! Queen or no queen, you shall die today!" Anokye threw a stone at the rooster.

The rooster dodged the stone and flew off toward the inner courts, crowing even louder.

Anokye chased after it, fuming. When he reached the inner courts, he found the rooster standing on top of the crate.

Anokye's gaze followed the bird. He prepared to throw his slipper at it. "Don't even think about—" His hand froze in midair.

The golden stool was gone.

CHAPTER 38

Suspicions

The steady beat of drums echoed throughout the Ashanti kingdom. The citizens of Ashanti knew the sounds of war.

Anokye rushed to the inner courts. "The stool is gone! The stool is gone!"

News spread quickly around the palace that King Kofi had declared a state of emergency. Warriors were dispatched all over the city. No one was allowed to leave. Merchants who had left the night before or in the early morning were chased down by scouts and forced to return. Everyone was considered guilty until the golden stool was found.

"Anokye!" the king shouted.

"Your Highness?" Anokye dared not meet the king's gaze.

"How did this happen?"

"Your Highness, I have no words. I was forcefully awoken by Akoko. It attacked me as if to alert me of the theft."

The rooster crowed loudly in acknowledgment.

"Summon Odom and the grand oracle at once," King Kofi growled to Anokye.

"Your Highness." Anokye bowed and hurried off.

191

King Kofi was not one to cower under pressure. He would not accept the loss of the venerated golden stool during his reign. It would destroy his legacy. He was ready to do whatever it took to recover the stool.

The warriors rushed to the Agamatsa Forest. A thick canopy of leaves prevented the light from reaching the forest floor.

The grand oracle, Akropo, lived at the top of Mount Afadja, which towered 2,905 feet above sea level. No one had seen him ascend or descend completely. At best, he had been seen ascending a mere hundred feet before disappearing. It was rumored that he had a secret stairway inside the mountain, but no one had been able to determine its veracity.

It would take days to climb the mountain and deliver the message to Akropo, several more days to descend, and even more time to reach the palace. They could not afford such a delay.

Odom had given instructions to the warriors before leaving the palace: "Climb the mountain until you see the smoke from Akropo's camp."

Odom and his troupe of Ashanti messengers reached the foot of the mountain.

The lead messenger retrieved a box from his comrade and climbed one hundred feet. He opened the box, pulled out a pigeon, and attached a message to its foot. Pigeons and ravens alike had been trained to fly long distances and deliver messages. The pigeon headed toward the smoke, and the group settled in to wait.

Warriors had headed in all directions the merchants went—to bring them back to the palace.

The group from Odùduwà, led by Iyìolá, had joined other caravans as they left the Ashanti kingdom. They stopped to rest close to the land of Ewe.

The Ewe people were relatively fewer in number than other tribes, but their location in the center of the Gbe region made them pivotal in interethnic affairs.

As the group neared the borders of Ewe, they heard a rustling in the bushes. Seconds later, Ashanti warriors sprang from the foliage.

"Stop! Do not move!" the leader of the platoon ordered.

Odom met Anokye in the outer court. "Old man, what have you done? This has never happened before!"

"Shut your mouth," Anokye snapped. "You were not even born when I began to watch over the stool."

Odom remained silent, not wanting to exacerbate the situation.

"The grand oracle shall shed light on this situation. Have you dispatched your men?"

"I have followed the king's orders," Odom replied brusquely. "My men are in the Agamatsa Forest as we speak."

"Odom!" King Kofi called.

Odom entered the king's court and bowed. "Your Highness."

"Your men have been dispatched?"

"Yes, Your Highness," Odom answered.

"What about the visitors? One of the groups is surely responsible for this." The king turned and sat on his throne.

"My men are rounding them up presently. They shall all return by nightfall. We shall get to the bottom of this matter, Your Highness."

"We shall see." King Kofi contemplated the ornate patterns on the court ceiling. "We shall see."

The warriors surrounded the caravans.

"What is this madness?" Iyìolá demanded. "Why have we been stopped in this manner?"

The warriors did not answer.

The merchants protested as the warriors ransacked their belongings. "What insolence! Why are you doing this?"

Iyìolá jumped to block one of the warriors from rummaging through the bags of money. "Do not touch that! It belongs to the king—"

The warrior brushed him aside. Gold and silver coins tumbled to the ground as he ripped the bag from Iyìolá's horse.

After a thorough search, the warriors stopped. They had not found what they were looking for.

The leader of the search party examined the group with a steely glare. "Which of you has the golden stool? If you do not produce it, none of you shall return home alive!"

"What are you talking about?" Iyìolá said.

"You are all returning to Ashanti with us. If you make one wrong move, it shall be your last before you meet your ancestors!"

"This is unbelievable. Absolutely unbelievable," Iyìolá stewed as the warriors prodded them back to the Ashanti kingdom.

Akropo approached the sleeping messengers. He stamped his staff on the floor, triggering a low rumble that shook the mountain.

The messengers awoke in a panic.

"Get up. Let us go to the king," Akropo stated without emotion. White paint circled his eyes. His long white beard was tied to his cane to prevent it from dragging on the floor. He proceeded down the mountain. The messengers slipped and stumbled as they tried to keep up. At the bottom of the mountain, Akropo strode directly toward the city center.

The warriors had rounded up all the merchants in the city square. They surrounded the parties, leaving no escape route.

The king stood to address the crowd. "The Ashanti kingdom has been gracious to you all. We have hosted you as we have done since the days of our ancestors. It seems that courtesy has been reciprocated with malevolence. One of you has stolen our sacred stool. That artefact is of paramount importance to the Ashanti people. If the stool is not produced, no one shall leave my kingdom alive."

194

The merchants eyed each other suspiciously, shocked by the accusation.

Akropo emerged from the crowd and bowed before the king. "Oh, King."

The crowd went silent at the sight of the grand oracle. Akropo's presence was intimidating. His brown wrapper was covered in dirt from living in the mountains without bathing. Even flies and mosquitoes avoided him.

"Great oracle." The king bowed to Akropo. Offending the oracle could lead to a curse that would ruin him.

"I have heard of the recent events. One of these merchants has the stool. We shall discover who the offenders are."

The people of Ashanti raised their voices, demanding an answer.

Akropo unwrapped his staff from his beard and threw it on the floor. It started to spin, and when it stopped, it started vibrating. Akropo took several steps toward the traders. He observed the orientation of the vibrating staff and stretched his arms wide. "One of these people has it." Akropo moved closer and pointed. "It is among these people." He looked at Odom.

Odom and five other warriors grabbed the two Portuguese men, Iyìolá, and two members of the caravan from Odùduwà.

The men screamed in protest as they were dragged away.

"What should we do with them, O great oracle?" King Kofi asked.

"You are king. I am an oracle. My work here is done." Akropo wrapped his beard around his staff. "The gods be with you!"

Everyone watched in silence as Akropo retreated into the forest.

CHAPTER 39

Salvation

Captain Manuel da Silva stood at the helm of *Aguas Negras*. The ship derived its name from being particularly reliable while sailing through storms. She had saved the captain from many tempests that had threatened the lives of him and his crew. The four white sails contrasted beautifully against the ship's wooden frame. She was a joy to the captain and all who sailed on her.

Vasco da Gama, a Portuguese explorer, had commissioned Captain da Silva's voyage after his own successful expedition around the Cape of Good Hope to India. He had met the people of Guinea in his travels, who were rich in both traditions and material wealth, and he hoped to secure more trade with the Guineans to benefit his homeland.

The Portuguese Empire was on the ascent, aided by the development of superior maritime technology. The Dark Continent seemed to have endless resources. Interaction with the Ashanti had been occurring for several years, and its gold was of prime importance. Although diplomacy was primary in gaining access to their resources and fostering trade, the unofficial modus operandi gave sway to any means necessary.

Pedro and Francisco had embarked on their first unsupervised expedition to trade with the Ashanti. They brought alcohol, guns, mirrors, and intricately made objects to trade with King Kofi. In exchange, they sought to obtain as much gold as possible. They were to attend the three-day market in Kumasi and return to the ship, but after more than a week, there was no sign of the men.

Food and water had been replenished, but if the crew stayed ashore too long, they would have to spend more money on supplies, which would detract from the profits. The financiers of the voyage were not known to have big hearts.

Captain da Silva approached two of his trusted sailors. "Luis! Ramon! Seek a guide to take you inland. Go and find out what is taking Pedro and Francisco so long. We can't wait for them indefinitely."

"Yes, Captain," they responded and headed off.

The sailors paid a local guide to lead them to the city. They inquired from locals around the city of the whereabouts of the two white merchants. Eventually, Luis and Ramon learned of the Portuguese sailors and others' arrests.

With the help of their local guide, they located the Ashanti palace. Once they arrived, Luis and Ramon were led into the palace. It was difficult not to marvel at the décor. Golden thread was wrapped around each pillar, and figurines made of gold and wood adorned the courts. Discs of solid gold hung from the ceiling. They dazzled magnificently when light fell on them. The wealth of the Ashanti kingdom was undeniable.

The king stood beside the throne, deep in conversation with his advisers, and he did not acknowledge the visitors.

The courtier started to speak, but King Kofi's hand flew up to silence him. After a brief moment, the king looked at the courtier. "What do you want?"

"Your Highness, the white men are here to see you."

"And what do they want?" the king asked impatiently. He walked over to his throne and sat.

The Portuguese sailors bowed before King Kofi and spoke through an interpreter.

Luis began, "Your Highness, we have heard that our brothers are being held prisoner as they have been accused of stealing a golden stool. We believe there must be some kind of mistake. Our fellow sailors are men of integrity. They are trustworthy. We have come to plead with you for their release so we can return to our ship together, Your Highness. We shall run out of supplies if we do not sail soon."

Ramon nodded in agreement.

"You want to take your brothers home?" the king exclaimed. "Tell them to return the stool, and they shall be set free!"

"Your Highness, we have traded with your kingdom for some time now. We have never violated your norms or laws. To arrest our men based on the testimony of your oracle is not something we can accept. There is no reason why our men would steal from you after successfully trading, Your Highness. We appeal to you to set our men free so we can continue a cordial and mutually beneficial relationship."

King Kofi stood up. He had participated in several meetings with foreign governments and was a strong negotiator. "I do not care what you think or feel about my decisions. I am king. And you come into my presence and disparage my oracle! Our traditions! And my people! What insolence. Get out!"

"But, Your Highness —"

"Leave at once, before I remove your heads from your shoulders!" King Kofi growled.

The courtiers shoved Luis and Ramon out of the palace and led them to a small holding room within the palace walls.

The prison windows faced the forest. Iyìolá gazed out at the landscape and speculated about the outcome of this predicament. Word had reached the prisoners that the Portuguese were attempting to secure their compatriots' release. Iyìolá knew that he was not guilty, and he had confidence in his men. These white men, on the other hand, were not people he could validate. The Portuguese sailors eyed the men from Odùduwà with equal suspicion.

Iyìolá decided to test the two foreigners. *Perhaps I can extract a confession from one of them.* "Francisco, let me tell you something. I have a man who can help you turn large pieces of solid gold into small nuggets."

Francisco looked at Iyìolá with suspicion. "What do you mean?"

Iyìolá replied, "I am saying that we can melt the gold—like the golden stool—and sell it to the Arabs."

Francisco walked away.

Iyìolá's Portuguese was broken, but as a trader, he had learned enough to conduct business. He approached Pedro. "We can work together. We could bribe the guards, and we could all walk away rich. Think about it. You shall have no need to continue sailing." He studied Pedro's aura. "You can even move to Odùduwà. Everything you need shall be provided for you."

One of the prison guards passed the cell and sneered. "Your kinsmen begged our king to release you, but he refused. You shall die here!" He laughed and walked away.

Later that evening, Pedro crawled to Iyìolá's corner. "How can you get us out of here?"

Aha! The moment of confession, Iyìolá thought. He addressed Pedro calmly. "Like I said earlier, I have a man who can convert the stool to golden nuggets. We shall make more money than we could ever imagine! Now, where is the stool?"

Pedro studied Iyìolá, debating whether he could trust him. Finally, he said, "Remember the last night of the market festival, during the celebration?"

Iyìolá nodded.

"After they unveiled the stool?"

"I remember," Iyìolá responded.

"In the middle of the night, when everyone was asleep …" Pedro explained how he and Francisco had stolen the precious relic. "But how do we deal with the king? He shall never release us if we say we took the stool."

"That is not a problem. I shall tell the king that one of these lowly men of mine took the stool. They shall punish him, and we shall go free. Trust me … this shall work out. Now, where is the stool?" Iyìolá gazed into Pedro's eyes.

Pedro shifted uncomfortably and then said, "It is on our ship. One of our fellow sailors hid it. Only he knows. If our captain finds out, we shall be in grave trouble."

I knew they would come clean. Iyìolá probed Pedro for details of the theft, and then he called to one of the guards and whispered in his ear.

The guard's eyes widened in shock, and he stormed out of the quarters.

A short while later, several guards came to the cell. "Out! You shall go before the king."

Iyìolá turned to the men who had come with him from Odùduwà. "I told you that we shall not die here. They shall release us soon."

The guards led the five prisoners to the king. Elders, advisers, and warriors were present, including extended members of the royal family.

"Bring the white men forward," King Kofi instructed the guards.

They were shoved in front of the king.

Anokye shot Francisco and Pedro a deathly glare. "So, you took the stool!" He shook his head.

King Kofi pointed his index finger menacingly at Francisco and Pedro and yelled with all his might, "You rogues! You shall not leave until you return the stool!" The king sat down in a huff and turned to Anokye. "And these pale foreigners said *we* were mad. They said that our grand oracle could not discern the truth."

The sailors glanced at Iyìolá, confused. Iyìolá had promised he would blame one of his merchants from Odùduwà. "We did not take the stool, Your Highness."

"Odom, take them back to jail. Every day, bring them out, tie them to poles in the market square, and give them as many lashes as you see fit until they tell us where the stool is." His countenance softened as he turned to Iyìolá. "I apologize for this misunderstanding. We shall keep you and your people in comfortable quarters until we have the stool in our possession."

Iyìolá bowed. "Your Highness."

The sailors were brought out the first day and lashed publicly. Their bodies were covered in red streaks, but their punishment yielded no confession.

On the second day, the men were lashed again, which created dark purple bruises that started to bleed. The third day produced flesh wounds, but the men refused to confess.

The king was beginning to doubt Iyìolá's testimony.

On the fourth day, when the guards went to the cell, Pedro did not stand. They kicked him, but he did not react. The guards called for the palace physician, and after he examined Pedro, he pronounced him dead.

When the message was delivered to the king, he summoned Francisco. "You have witnessed the fate of your brother. I assure you that you shall die a similar death!"

Francisco finally broke down and said, "Your Highness, we took the stool."

Gasps of shock and shouts of rage erupted from the crowd.

"Where is it?" the king thundered.

"It is on our ship, Your Highness. One of our comrades stowed it in the hull. No one else knows about it, Your Highness." Francisco fell to the floor, sobbing. Malnourishment and severe beatings had weakened him so much that he could barely stand.

Odom summoned warriors and charged to the shore where the Portuguese ship was docked.

Manuel da Silva had just finished his morning prayers and was putting on his uniform when Odom and his men arrived.

Odom shouted, "Captain da Silva, one of your men has confessed to taking the golden stool! I am here to retrieve it."

The captain emerged from his room and climbed the stairs to the ship's deck.

The sailors aboard the ship had their muskets pointed at the Ashanti warriors.

This is going to be an eventful day, Da Silva thought.

"We cannot let you aboard our ship," Captain da Silva said as the Ashanti warriors attempted to board. "We shall inquire of our men where the stool was kept, and we shall retrieve it on your behalf. But, again, you cannot traverse this ship. Otherwise, there shall be bloodshed, and I doubt it shall be that of my men."

"Very well." Odom turned to one of his high-ranking warriors. "Go and bring the sailors here—including the dead one."

The warrior rode off.

The remaining Ashanti warriors set up camp on the beach directly in front of the ship. No Portuguese would leave without their permission.

On the evening of the second day, the warrior arrived with forty more men, as well as Francisco, Luis, and Ramon. Pedro's limp body was draped over a horse near the rear of the procession.

"Captain da Silva, we have your men," Odom announced. "They shall tell you where the stool is. You shall give us our stool, and we shall give you back your men."

"Where is the stool, Francisco?" Captain da Silva demanded.

"It is in the hull, Captain," Francisco replied quietly. "Guillermo, go get the stool."

Guillermo looked both surprised and fearful. Their plan had been exposed.

Captain da Silva looked at Guillermo with disbelief as he quietly led the captain to where they had hidden the stool. Captain da Silva asked his men to retrieved it. He approached the Ashanti with his men carrying the sacred stool. They set it down unceremoniously on the sand.

Two Ashanti men rushed to pick up the stool.

Odom gasped in horror. "Captain, after all your men have done, you now dare to put our stool on the ground? You have no understanding of the curse you may bring upon yourself!"

The sailors' hands flew to their daggers, and they moved in front of their captain, ready to defend him.

The Ashanti warriors followed suit, holding their daggers and spears, and the four accompanying archers took their positions.

"Where is the other man? Where is Pedro?" Captain Da Silva asked.

"Bring him," Odom directed.

Two men went to the back of the line, pulled the body off the horse, placed it on a bamboo stretcher, and brought it forward. He was covered in a dusty linen from head to toe. They dropped him in front of the captain.

The captain's eyes widened as he uncovered the face of the figure. It was Pedro. "What happened to him?" he demanded.

"Ask his comrade, Francisco," Odom replied smugly. "I'm sure he can explain. They brought this upon themselves."

On both sides, daggers and spears remained poised for battle.

Da Silva raised his hands. "There shall be no fighting today."

"Very well." Odom sheathed his dagger and turned to leave.

"I am not finished, sir," da Silva said. "You killed one of my men."

Odom turned to face da Silva. "Your man committed a treacherous crime against the Ashanti people. He deserved death and more."

Da Silva glowered at Odom. "This shall not go unanswered. I hope you understand that." We shall seek retribution—that is a promise."

"Looking forward to it, white devil. Looking forward to it." Odom sneered. "No matter how early a child wakes in the morning, the tree stumps shall always be at the farm before he arrives." He made a full turn with his horse and rode off into the forest with his warriors, chanting battle cries.

The Portuguese sailors looked on as they disappeared into the thick jungle.

CHAPTER 40

Message to Ashanti

Two days had passed since Odùduwà had sent their emissaries to Dahomey. King Àjosè was seated in the king's court, wondering why the messengers were taking so long. He stared into the distance. *I hope Dahomey supports our course against Hawani.*

Dòngárì hurried into the court, interrupting the king's thoughts. He knelt on one knee with his hand on his chest. "Your Highness, the messengers are back!"

King Àjosè's eyes lit up. "Let them in!"

The messengers prostrated before the king. "Your Highness." Their downcast expressions were not encouraging.

"What did King Drogba say?"

The messengers looked at each other.

"What did he say?" King Àjosè bellowed. "Cat caught your tongues?"

The lead messenger stepped forward and handed Àjosè the note from Dahomey.

King Àjosè took the note and read it. "So, he turned us down." The king nodded at the messengers and dismissed them. "Thank you for your service." King Àjosè remained seated on his throne, considering his next strategic move.

Iyìolá returned to Odùduwà with his fellow merchants, and after the guards ushered them into the king's presence, they delivered their acquired goods and narrated the harrowing experience as prisoners in the Ashanti dungeon.

The king consoled them, appeased them with gifts, and sent them home. He mulled over the events in Kumasi. King Àjosè was known to be diplomatic and carefully considered his actions before making a move. "Dòṅgárì!"

"My king?"

"Bring me a writing feather, a jar of ink, and a clean cloth!"

"Yes, Your Highness." Dòṅgárì quickly returned with the items.

"I want you to write down this message." The king told the other messengers to leave the room.

Dòṅgárì dipped the feather into the small jar of ink, his hand poised to record Àjosè's exact words on the linen cloth.

The king paced back and forth. "Greetings from the kingdom of Odùduwà. Your Highness, I am saddened to learn of the theft of your sacred golden stool. It has come to my attention that Iyìolá, our representative, and others from Odùduwà were detained due to this issue." Àjosè paused for a few seconds. "I am glad to learn that the thieves who carried out this unthinkable act have now been caught—and that my people have been exonerated.

"King Guguwa of Hawani has declared war against the Odùduwà kingdom. I understand that my request may not be appropriate under the present circumstances in your kingdom. However, if you join forces with us against the Hawani kingdom, we shall join forces with you against the white men to avenge the theft of your ancient golden stool. It is my hope and belief that we can maintain this good relationship beyond these difficult times." King Àjosè took the note from Dòṅgárì, dipped his royal seal in red-hot wax, stamped the bottom of the white piece of linen, and wrapped it.

"Summon the messengers at once," the king said.

"Your Highness." Dòngárì bowed and hurried off. He returned within the hour with three messengers.

King Àjosè handed the note to the lead messenger. "Set out for the Ashanti kingdom before sunrise tomorrow. Give this letter to King Kofi when you arrive. May our ancestors be with you."

The lead messenger bowed with his hand to his chest. "My king."

CHAPTER 41

Vespera Da Destruicao

In Kumasi, the blades of grass moved almost imperceptibly in the morning breeze. The morning sun was halfway to its crest. A few chickens strutted outside the palace walls. Akoko was among them, gingerly leading a small procession of chicks across a dusty path.

The palace was a shadow of what it had been during the celebrations; there was nothing festive about the current situation. The golden stool had been placed in a reinforced cage in the inner sanctum, which was below ground level. Day and night, two warriors guarded the entrance to the inner sanctum.

The Odùduwà messengers arrived at the Ashanti kingdom, and guards took them to King Kofi.

Anokye stood beside King Kofi.

King Kofi read King Àjosè's letter carefully. *Hmm. I could use King Àjosè and his kingdom to help me fight the white men who may bring war to our doorstep.* King Kofi quickly dictated a letter to his scribe and stamped it with his own royal seal. "Tell Àjosè we shall stand with him. Please reiterate our apologies for the detention of his people. I am sure he, of all people, shall understand our error."

The messenger bowed and departed.

207

Anokye pondered the recent occurrences surrounding the golden stool. "Your Highness, the Portuguese promised there would be retribution. How shall we defend our kingdom?"

"We shall post scouts on the beach to watch for activity. We must be vigilant since our military shall be divided between defending Ashanti and allying with Odùduwà against Hawani. We have given our word to King Àjosè; hence we must oblige him. These strategic alliances are necessary. We shall need Odùduwà in the future."

King Guguwa stood on the parapet of his castle's southern wall. He pointed toward Odùduwà, talking to himself. "We shall commence our march toward Odùduwà tonight. We shall take them by surprise. There shall be no warning. We shall overrun the homes of the vermin. We shall make them pay for their insolence! There shall be a new dawn for Hawani."

In the field below, Àmínù paced back and forth on Baruwa, his black stallion. Baruwa was magnificent; he stood a full hand above most other horse. His coat and mane shone like a well-polished obsidian stone, and the sunlight etched intricate patterns on his muscles.

Àmínù was a sight to behold in his white battle gear. He inspired his army and struck fear in his enemies. Baruwa trotted quickly as Àmínù surveyed his army.

The army let out loud shouts and screams. The archers were positioned in front, and the horsemen were behind. Hawani's cavalry would surely challenge Odùduwà. The infantry stood behind the horsemen. Odùduwà's infantry was vicious, but Àmínù had a plan.

Word traveled fast through neighboring towns and villages. A network of messengers loyal to Odùduwà passed the news from village to village.

Dòngárì kept up with news in the region. He received the message that King Guguwa was to embark on his journey toward Odùduwà that night and sent a messenger to Àjàmú.

The messenger reached Àjàmú's hut. "My lord, Dòngárì has sent me. Hawani is marching tonight!"

Àjàmú rushed to the palace and bowed hastily. "My king, I understand that Hawani is marching toward Odùduwà tonight.

"That is correct, General. Àmínù the Madawaki is leading the charge. Did you not face him years ago when you were a boy?" Àjosè asked.

Àjàmú nodded.

"A most formidable opponent, that one, but you have faced worse. You and I have defeated many Àmínùs!"

"Yes, we have, Your Highness. Yes, we have," Àjàmú replied. "But they are not known to play fair."

"Then we must have a solid plan." The king paused to think. "With a large army, Hawani shall need about seven days to get here. Hence, we shall leave tomorrow morning."

"I agree, my king. Let them draw close enough to our territory to give them the illusion of control—but not so deep that they may take our land. We shall then draw them into the forest and unleash our attack."

King Àjosè stroked his beard. "How far into our territory should we allow them to advance before the first contact?"

"The forest near the Arinta waterfall in Èjìgbò, my king. We must stop them before they cross the Òpá River. We shall prepare to ambush them there. Hawani shall have archers, but we shall send our archers and armored men in the front to counter theirs. We shall coordinate with the Ashantis and prepare to secure more allies, if need be." Àjàmú paused to ensure he had King Àjosè's full attention.

The king nodded.

Àjàmú continued, "We shall also leave a contingency force in Èjìgbò and nearby cities. We cannot exhaust our entire military with the first battle."

"Very well, General. This is a good plan. Send word to the Qbas (kings), and send another message to Dahomey. They must be alerted, lest the battle draw close to their territory unannounced. However, as soon as this is over, I shall deal with Drogba myself. They shall pay a huge price for their insolence and disloyalty. At twilight tomorrow, we move. Tell the men to enjoy their last night with their wives and children." He wanted to prove that he was as great a warrior as his father and that he would put down any insurrection. It would not be said that the great kingdom of Odùduwà fell under his rule.

Àjàmú sent a raven to Dahomey to alert them of war near their borders.

King Drogba called his advisers, Queen Témbè and Princess Fazilah, Ológun, and the leaders of the male contingent. "The time has come for us to prepare for war. If Odùduwà wins this war, Àjosè may set his sights on Dahomey."

It would be nearly impossible to conquer Odùduwà, but after fighting Hawani and its allies, Odùduwà would be weak enough for Dahomey to put up a strong resistance. Odùduwà would not be able to defeat Dahomey, which would force them to sign a truce.

If the two kingdoms brokered such an accord, King Drogba would uphold it. Despite his faults, he was a man of honor. Odùduwà and Dahomey were bound together by the Yorùbá culture, which had forged a certain degree of mutual respect between the kingdoms despite the tensions.

Queen Témbè said, "My king, I shall send word to my people, but Abyssinia is far away. They may not see it fit to involve themselves in a far-off battle, but they may send supplies."

King Drogba nodded to his wife in appreciation. "A conflict with Odùduwà may be inevitable. Generals! Ológun! Keep your ears to the ground. Maybe Lúlù shall finally be of use to us."

Princess Fazilah looked up at the mention of Lúlù. She did not want her new friend dragged into this conflict: she had a baby to tend to.

At sunrise, the Dahomey army, including the Mino, began training.

The Hawani army was only a five-day ride from Èjìgbò.

Àjàmú spurred his horse forward as the warriors ran through the Èjìgbò Forest. They were a few hours from the Arinta waterfall. They

210

had to cross the Òpá River and reach the waterfall to prepare for the ambush.

In the Ashanti kingdom, King Kofi had prepared his army to march. He had received word that it would be fought in the northern highlands of Odùduwà. It would take at least one week to arrive at the battlefield. He sent only half of his army; the other half would remain to protect his homeland.

"The gods be with you." King Kofi touched Odom's head with his golden staff.

"Your Highness." Odom bowed and went to meet his men outside the palace.

An Ashanti scout perched in a tree on the shore, almost a day's journey from Kumasi, noticed an object on the horizon. *Perhaps it is a mirage.* The scout broke open a coconut, drank the water, and dozed off.

A few minutes later, he awoke with a start, almost falling from the tree. He examined the horizon again. It was not a mirage. In the distance, he spotted white sails. "One, two, three, four, five, six, seven, eight, nine, ten ships. Ten ships!" The scout gasped.

They were Portuguese ships. Captain da Silva had kept his word.

The scout jumped down, clambered onto his horse, and galloped toward the palace.

War drums beat throughout the empires. News of the impending battles spread like wildfire. The elders stared at the horizon as the sounds of war reverberated through the land.

The curses of the gods and oracles had begun to manifest. The extended period of peace in the motherland had been replaced by turmoil. The future was uncertain for the warring kingdoms and for many others in close proximity. Blood, it seemed, would soon eclipse the sun. And so it began—the many more challenges, struggles, and wars of the motherland.

Made in United States
Orlando, FL
01 December 2023

39933773R00136